SINS OF THE MOTHERS

"Dennis Carey's multiple-layered, mu
return to Templeboy, County Sligo wii
that part of the world. There, the power of family and of events past and present will take you from decades past to the present day within the context of a full and rich tapestry of Irish life.

Carey's efficient writing weaves both light and shade into his storytelling, through the innocence of first love, to the darkness of relationships torn apart. From flashback to the here and now you'll be taken on a journey the like of which you'll not want to interrupt for a moment." **John Griff - BBC Radio**

"A terrific read! A great book should leave you with many experiences and a little exhausted. Sins of the Mothers *fits into this category and is compelling reading from start to finish.*

Although the story is fictitious, the locations are real enough and brought back many happy memories for me of my childhood days in Sligo and neighbouring Mayo. I'm sure this will be the case for many. Those who have never been there will be keen to visit.

Paul is in search of a mother forced to give him up for adoption many decades earlier by the Irish authorities. I was eager to learn whether or not there is a happy ending and if mother and son eventually come together from opposite ends of the world.

Ireland in the fifties and sixties was a very different place from that of today. The Catholic Church ruled its people with an iron fist and fear was the order of the day. Unmarried mothers were not accepted and were hidden away in Irish Mother and Baby Homes, in most cases never to be united with their families again. Carey's book captures the sad legacy of the recently reported findings of mass children's graves in those care homes."

Henry Wymbs – Author, presenter of BBC's *Irish Eye.*

Sins of the Mothers

By Dennis Carey

Published by Dennis Martin Carey

Sins of the Mothers

A CIP catalogue record for this book is
available from the British Library.

ISBN 978-0-9931943-3-7

To Carol
Thank you for the
support.
Very best wishes
Dennis Carey
Jan 2018

iii

The adopted and their mothers.

1

I watched him exit customs.

He dropped his carryall, stood astride his luggage and stretched long arms wide, bending back his spine. I imagined his sternum clicking a release.

He was tall, my height but leaner. The bronzed face looked younger than its thirty-nine years, though lustered and drawn from the long journey. The jawline was square, shadowed by bristle but still sharply prominent right back to beneath the ears.

His features would fill any mother with pride. There would be tears too, tears of joy, of regret, and a clinging prodigal embrace for a long-lost son. His mother would be proud, but his mother wasn't there. And he didn't know who his mother was.

The dark-chestnut hair was cropped short, tidy, almost military. He reminded me of a particular type of prison inmate, the gym freak, rangy and drained from killing too much time on the treadmill. Tanned, muscled calves were visible beneath well-tailored shorts. County Mayo, in the rainy west of Ireland, and he wore short trousers. Not how I expected a businessman to dress.

He unfolded a mobile telephone and spoke into it while darting his gaze around the arrivals hall. He checked his watch, stared people in the face as they passed, bounced on his feet. Though born of this land, he was a stranger to it.

I turned away when he glanced in my direction. I'd meet him on my terms. When I was ready. When I was good and ready.

2

Seven months before Paul McDonnell's plane descended through navy-grey clouds to land at Knock International Airport, I clicked opened an email.

> From: Paul McD
> Date: 11 February 1997, 8:03am
> Subject: Your book

> *Just started reading The Harvester, enjoying it so far. Bought it because my birth mum lives in Sligo, a single mum in 1958. I was adopted out. Living in Australia nearly 40 years. We've had no contact since. Believe her husband had something to do with the peat industry. Keen to read the book and learn more about that part of the world. Never been back to Ireland but intend to go there soon to search for my birth mum. I've been thinking about her a lot in recent years.*

The Harvester, my first novel. 96,000 words, 1900 hours of research, writing, editing, re-writing, checking the research, re-writing. Book published. Though equivalent to forty weeks of full-time work, it took nearly forty years to write.

I first had the idea at the age of eighteen and shelved it next to my other teenage plans: train in mechanical engineering, sail a ship, hold up Coventry's Corporation Street branch of the Midland Bank, and travel the world evading the police.

Plans not discarded remained on that shelf when I started work. Not easy, writing a book whilst holding down a full-time job. I'd arrive home, at any-time o'clock, ready to snap the neck of anyone who got between me and my first drink. Both ex-wives can vouch for that.

Blame the drinking on the extraordinary stresses of prison officer work. In case anyone was to ask, that's the excuse I armed myself with. No-one asked.

Her Majesty's Prison Service introduced me to humankind's dangerous, hateful and vengeful. I recall cutting down a suicidal rapist, night shift, first on the scene, in the early hours. The yells from prisoners, glowering faces pressed against metal grills, made it clear they wished it was I who dangled from the railing. Such enmity was typical. I fought back with sarcasm, provoking taunts and belittling jibes, the tools of my trade necessary, I was sure, to coerce and control my charges. After a shift of that, I never thought about sitting down to pen a novel.

The psychoanalyst who probed my head with open questions said, "The repulsion slowly builds in you."

I disagreed. It tidal-waved over me. Landing 2A, D wing, late on a Wednesday evening. I was careless, stupid even. I ran to rescue an inmate I recognised from the lower landing, a timid man, nervy and overtly homosexual, vulnerable in the setting of a high-security prison. He was shoved through a doorway, and I reacted. The young man was bait. The sardonic bastard kissed me on the mouth before he left the cell.

There were three of them, Vinceman the ringleader and by far the more terrifying. Vinceman scared me. *Really* scared me. I had never seen hate like the hate hoarded in those dark, grey eyes. Hate with a blade, death a steeled slice away.

In his investigative report on the incident, the Prisons and Probation Ombudsman, Nigel Hesseltine, OBE, concluded I was "irresponsible".

I drank again. I mean *really* drank. The way I used to each time a wife left me. Worse, even. When the report was published I was barely sober enough to read it. I stopped working. Couldn't work. People scared me. I stayed in my flat. On my own.

3

Few believed it possible, I didn't believe it possible, but where mule-drawn carts once sank to their axles in a hilltop bog aeroplanes now taxied on a tarmac runway. By the time Paul McDonnell's plane landed at Knock International, Ireland's most implausible airport, the tip of my thumb bled from over-biting.

My flight from Birmingham, the middle of England, had landed two hours earlier. I hired a car. The alcohol was a risk, but it calmed me. The head-woman told me during a consultation, "Your problem is you use one illness to treat the other." I dismissed her quackery. Told her, "You know shit about me."

I gulped back the last of my whiskey, felt it invade me, the burn tearing at the knot of nerves in my stomach. I took two steady breaths, stepped out from behind the pillar in the corner of the cramped bar, and strode towards him.

"Got to go," Paul McDonnell said into the handset. "Sit tight, I'll sign them when I'm back." He smiled in recognition, his teeth white and straight. He flipped the telephone closed and palmed the fragile aerial home. "It's the author!" He opened his arms as to embrace. "We meet at last. How you goin'?"

I stood back from him.

He hesitated, then flashed his mobile phone at me and tucked it in a pocket of his jacket. "Lettin' folks know I landed."

"You're late," I said. Not the greeting I planned.

His eyebrows flickered. "You're right. I apologise. Lucky the London connection was delayed or it would've been tomorrow. Some poor bastard missed final boardin' in Sydney. We sat on the apron over an hour while they dug his bags out the hold."

He grinned. "Thought the drinks trolley'd never get green lighted. Still nervous on planes."

I jerked my head at the rapid speech, sentences pared to the last, and clipped antipodean accent. How could I not have expected it? Act confident. I extended a hand. Talk confident. "Are you still prepared to go through with this?"

He pumped my clammy hand up and down, his grip firm and dry, and leaned in. "Didn't fly twenty-four hours to kiss a Blarney stone." He winked a tired blue eye. "Another drink? Owe you one for keepin' you waitin'."

Was he testing me? "We need to get on," I said.

Thick ribbons of rain fell in crackling splashes from the sloping asbestos roof of a large open barn. Beneath its shelter, Paul gave a cursory glance at my selection of hire car, a Micra, and asked the attendant if an upgrade was possible.

The attendant straightened, rested his hands on his hips and smiled. "What're ya thinkin'?"

"BMW?" Paul said.

"We've better than that. Audi two-point-four V6. Just arrived. They do a two-point-eight but the gobshites won't let me order one in. Will I get it out for ya?"

Paul paid the price difference with a credit card.

"Thought it'd be greener," Paul said.

We were high up, the clouds such an apocalyptic graphite grey I expected four horsemen to leap the car. The land lay below us in a splinter-camouflage quilt of khaki, a sepia hundred-year-old photograph, blurred by balloon-sized drops that diagonally overpowered the wipers. My mood soured.

"It is green," I said above the din of rain on the car roof.

"As much brown and black as green."

"That blanket of peat's older than Australia." My tone was sharp. "Formed when your country was populated by a few primitive hunter-gatherers with a belief system based on Dreamtime." I was over-defensive.

Paul was quiet.

"It rains here," I said, half explanation, half apology. "Every bloody day." I concentrated on driving drunk down the side of the hill, away from the airport.

The journey through the downpour to Ballyhaunis was short. Paul made a tentative suggestion we go for the drink he owed me, in town. It was still early evening, mindful of my morning appointment, I told him we would check-in at the bed and breakfast first.

Bridie Griffiths, our host, welcomed us as though we were old friends. We declined the offer of tea and soda bread. At Paul's request, she telephoned for a taxi.

"Tell me this," Mrs Griffiths said. "Do all the men wear short trousers in Australia?"

"We do when it's summer, Mrs G," Paul said, and laughed.

"Australian summers mustn't be like Irish summers," Mrs Griffiths said, laughing back.

I avoided eye contact and fidgeted inside my pocket, folding a twenty-euro note into a tiny rectangle. The whiskey boosted my confidence. "I thought I read this bed and breakfast is within walking distance of town."

Mrs Griffiths tutted. "Does it still say that?" She turned to a miniature hurl that hung on a small chain and plucked two key fobs off hooks screwed into it.

Paul smiled. "Don't worry about it, the taxi'll be fine."

"As sure as there's a God in heaven," Mrs Griffiths continued, "I've asked the booking people to change that several times. Sure, you couldn't walk in this weather anyhow, you'd be drowned." She rested the fingers of a hand on Paul's arm. "You in your shorts, an' all. Thomas'll take you in, and he'll bring you out whenever you want." She leaned into Paul. "He does all the taxiing for my guests. He'll be up for you now in a minute. Here're your keys, I won't wait up."

4

"You're a chronic alcoholic who's using the alcohol to treat the PTSD." The psychoanalyst jotted a brief note in the pad balanced on her knee. "Post-traumatic stress disorder," she said in response to my blank expression. She diagnosed me on the morning of my fiftieth birthday, four months after I left work. "Only the best people get it," she added and smiled. A thank-God-it's-not-me smile. I wanted to punch her and get drunk.

I didn't punch her, I did get drunk. For another year, maybe more. My progression was black Guinness, to wooing amber whiskey, then anything. I used mouthwash to disguise the smell, then swallowed bottles of it for the back-of-the-throat alcohol burn. When money ran out, I scavenged in bins for the dregs of discarded beer bottles. A fellow drunk taught me to suck the clear liquid from settled Kaolin and Morphine, an over-the-counter medicine I took to treat the diarrhoea. When there was nothing else, absolutely nothing else, and I was too sick or too drunk to leave the flat, I drank my own alcohol-infused vomit.

I know of an old man in County Sligo who sold a lump of land for sixty-five thousand euros. Within nine months, he had drunk most of the money and a necrotic pancreas poisoned him to death. Not having the pounds-sterling equivalent of sixty-five thousand euros to drink might have saved my life.

I didn't come through unscathed. Teeth fell from diseased and corroded gums, starting an obsession, I failed to attend a family funeral, and my vital organs were overwhelmed to the point of collapse. Addiction also isolates, acquaintances turned away, frustrated, trading contact for sobriety. I sank into a black pit of fear and depression so deep the opening above me narrowed to a pinprick of light. A victim of my own excess.

And then there were the nightmares. And the flashbacks.

The vagrant who introduced me to the foul-tasting morphine hit suggested a dog to care for would give my life purpose. From somewhere, I found the sense to return the long-eared Basset Hound to the refuge after a week.

I lacked the spirituality to benefit from an alcoholics' support group who introduced me to a twelve-step recovery programme. I had sunk too deep for only twelve steps. I needed a rope.

Writing was my rope, its heavy coil cast into the pit by the analyst. She encouraged me to write about Ireland. "We need to tackle your aversions," she said, "but we'll start with what you know. I like to call it 'Therapy of the Familiar'."

I took my book down from the shelf and wrote it. Eighteen months of isolated writing, the tremors in my fingers steadied each morning by only a single drink. I developed an irrational sensitivity to events in the news during that time, so closed myself off. Dunblane, royal divorces, the cloning of a sheep, all passed me by unnoticed. But I climbed from the depths, hand over hand, paragraph over paragraph, towards that pinprick light. December 1996 and it's done.

A bit on the book will help. It's about a boy aspiring to work with his father in the Irish peat industry. A company called Bord na Móna carried out industrialised extraction of peat from bogs in selected parts of the country. A regard for the biodiversity impact discourages them from doing that today, but the depressed 1950s was a different time in Ireland. Jobs and economic independence from England were more imperative than the preservation of a two-thousand-year-old natural habitat.

Anyway, early in the decade, Bord na Móna established a peat bog just outside the city of Sligo, in the northwest of Ireland. I worked there for a few months. My father worked there too. He drove a harvester machine, a rickety, dystopian monstrosity held together by metal pins, ropes, and the power of prayer. That's where I got the title, *The Harvester*. Never start a book title with the word 'The', they said. I ignored them.

5

Thomas took five minutes to drive as many miles, on a wet road, from our accommodation to the centre of Ballyhaunis town. He slid to a halt outside The High Court public house on Main Street. "You'll get a great feed in there," he said. "What time'll you want the lift back?"

I had an interview arranged for the following morning, my first book-promoting interview.

"About twelve, Tommo?" Paul said leaning his head between ours from the back seat. His breath smelled of stale beer. "Can you do twelve, we'll meet you here?"

"I can do twelve, alright," Thomas said. "And one, too."

"No!" I said. Rain tapped against the windscreen. I lowered my voice. "Twelve's late enough. How much do we owe you?"

Paul shuffled in his seat to get a hand into a pocket.

"Don't put a bother on yerself now, the way out's fine. Have a blast of a night lads, and I'll meet you at midnight. Stay dry."

Paul had entered the bar by the time I clambered out of the car. With a salute, Thomas accelerated away. I kept my hand aloft and splayed my wet fingers. The tremor was only slight. I took two deep breaths and leaned against the pub door.

"I've ordered you a pot of the black stuff," Paul said.

"I'd rather have–"

"Do you bloody good, mate. Whiskey'll rot yer gut. Like drinkin' car fuel. Seen it happen too often with folk."

I wasn't sure I wanted to be his mate. And was it that obvious I'd been drinking whiskey?

"Managed decent tickets on the flight," he said. "Did I tell you? Free bubbly all the way over to London if you don't mind.

Guinness and champers, ever tried it? Nice to be able to relax on a flight for a—"

"Now then, that's lovely." The tiny barmaid reached to place the drinks on the counter. She too was lovely, pale and freckled skin, fern-green eyes. Hair the rich colour of flax seed clasped in wisps high on her head. Her smile had a warmth that made you feel you were where you should be. A striking Irish beauty of contrasts.

She noticed Paul notice.

"Will ye be wantin' food, lads?" she said and tilted her head, a smiling angel. On her neck, a tiny tattoo of a bird with long tail-streamers took flight from its clavicle perch.

"Eatin's cheatin'," Paul said, reaching for his pint. "You've heard that one over here, right?"

The angelic barmaid widened her smile indulgently.

Clouds of brown bubbles surged and settled in my drink. My first Guinness in two years. "We'll have something," I said.

"That's lovely. Sit where ye like, I'll bring the menus. There's a specials board round the corner, lads, but if you want moussaka, you'll have a long wait, we're out of it 'til tomorra." Her grin beamed between the beer pumps. She had good teeth.

Paul laughed too generously.

Her eyes shifted and she said, "Ciarán, how are ya?"

The door behind me rattled closed. A young man, leaning to let rain drip from his waxed coat, ran a hand through wet hair.

"Good to see ya," the barmaid said. "Been a while."

Ciarán unbuttoned his coat. "And good to see you, Swal."

She moved nearer the counter. "What can I do for ya?"

"You can pull me a pint, will ya?"

"Pull somethin' else for ya, too," she said. The angelic demeanour disappeared, the halo slipped.

Ciarán glanced me a grin and winked, tying me into the exchange. He enjoyed the attention. "Still the tease, Swallow?"

She giggled and filled a glass. "Not in here for weeks and you're out on a night like this. Is it in to see me you are?"

"I wouldn't be gettin' in here much anymore." Another wink.
"Why?"

"No money." A smile.

"Feck right off," Swallow said. "Aren't you stupid-rich-caked in the stuff? Daddy owning half of Roscommon." Swallow placed the pint on the counter and rested an elbow beside it. She looked earnest. "So have ya any news?"

"No news."

"No news is good news," Swallow said.

I encouraged Paul to choose a table and excused myself.

Braced over the toilet bowl, I took stock. I'd survived the flight and the airports; hired a car, only to have my selection overruled; met Paul, not sure if I envied or despised his confidence; and checked into our accommodation. I'd also walked off the street into a pub. It had been a few years since I last managed that without getting evicted.

I felt relaxed. Whilst total abstinence was too tough a line to toe, I needed to keep a control of my drinking. I smiled. Therapy of the familiar. Familiar Ireland. The challenges of the trip seemed surmountable. I pulled the chain and raced the flush.

As I reached our table, Paul was weaving his way back from the counter with two more settling pints. He shouted over his shoulder, "Yourself, Swallow. And one for your friend, please."

"I've not started the first one," I said.

"What you think of Swallow?" he asked smiling. "There's not even any moussaka *on* the specials board." He pulled a stool under himself.

"And I should have bought these."

"No worries. Listen. This is bloody fantastic." Paul arranged his long legs. "I've been wantin' to do this for nine years. Nine bloody years, and here I am, in Ireland, doin' it. And it's thanks to you. I'm grateful. Wouldn't do it on my own." He raised his glass off the table. His wide eyes were damp. "And I'm lookin' forward to Templeboy. Even if it does rain every day. Sláinte, mate."

6

As a lad, growing up in Templeboy in County Sligo, I took comfort from the rain that came at night, the drops tapping the roof and rattling against the windowpane. I'd lay in bed, safe in the knowledge that no-one, other than, perhaps, Widow McCuff, would be prowling in such weather. Even the wizened Widow McCuff was harmless enough if you gave her a handful of potatoes from Mammy's basket, or a small head of cabbage. In exchange, she'd hand you a damp sprig of lucky heather and be on her way.

If it rained at night, I reasoned, the sky would wring the clouds dry of water before the day came. I hated rainy days.

There had been no rain for weeks.

That night it came with a vengeance, battering down like a fall of stone chippings onto the corrugated metal roof-sheets and buffeting the windowpanes in windy gusts.

I sat up in the bed with my younger brother, Sean, while the rain fell in recurrent crescendos. In the blackness, I prayed to God that the rusty roof edge above the back door would hold fast.

"Will ya go for one of the new jobs?" my mother said, down in the kitchen, her voice raised above the din of the elements. "God knows any money'd be handy, sure the farm's useless."

Bord na Móna was two years into the development of its site, and village talk was that work was ahead of schedule. Fine weather had allowed the bog to be topped and drained enough to begin harvesting peat a year early. Recruitment posters went up.

The concussive pound of my father's fist on the kitchen table boomed through the clatter of the rainfall. "No!"

I wrapped an arm around Sean. He drew in his little legs and tightened his shoulders. We both knew it wasn't the farm that was useless.

My father shouted, "Why in the name of feck would I do that?" Drunken words, slurred and severe. "Haven't I enough to do saving me own turf?"

Sean tucked his face into his knees.

I pulled him tight and kissed his hair.

"The farm'll look after us," my father said, quieter.

"Then you'll have to look after the farm."

The rain stopped. Silence. I closed my eyes and waited for my father's fury. More silence.

The scrape of a chair. The rising musical tone of water from a bucket filling a kettle. The metal on metal of the kettle on the hob.

"If I take a job, it'll be my decision."

I let my breath escape.

The faint splash of poitín in an upturned bottle.

In the middle of the night, a full bladder roused me from sleep. I lifted Sean's arm and slid out of the bed.

Two years earlier, a gang of Electricity Supply Board men pulled a cable through Templeboy in the rural electrification of Ireland, yet my father still preferred the shadowy glow of a candle. A lonely, gnarled specimen sat sentinel in the middle of the kitchen table. It shone a yellow halo, and sooty smoke wriggled from its tip. As I crossed the cold and worn patch of linoleum, my shadow rushed past over the wall and waited for me at the door. I lifted the latch. Disturbed air flickered the flame. I heard splashing though the rain had long gone. My father's narrow back materialised out of the blackness, the seat of his long johns swaying back and forth. I took up position beside him.

He had little Irish but said, "Uisce beatha, son. The monks' water of life…And look, like all life, it ends up in the ground."

13

I said nothing but joined him in the splashing.

"When you're lonely in love, son, the poitín is a warming wooer. Not hoor, now, wooer." He chuckled. "Sorry, son."

I frowned at the ground, tired and confused. Splashes of warmth speckled my cold toes.

"If you've money, the whiskey can woo too." My father held back his laughter at his wordplay. "But the poitín is the main man." He released his mirth in a cackle, his body flexing. "Not a hoor," he squeaked. When he laughed loudly into the darkness, his exaggerated sway threatened to fold him in the middle.

I shifted a foot off an annoying sharp stone.

"Your mother wants me to get a job," he whispered, serious and still. "Never begged for work in me life."

I finished.

He kept going, his man's bladder the size of a milk churn.

I turned back to the yellow glow of the candle and the warmth of my bed. "Night, Daddy."

"Uisce beatha, son…," he said, his voice flat. "You can rely on the water of life."

"Ish-ga bah-hah," I repeated, my fate determined.

My mother laid out his best clothes.

She checked the alignment of his collar and cap and hovered her nose in the air whilst he grumbled at the attention. He hadn't touched the poitín that morning.

On his return, my father gave us the news that he had managed to convince the Bord na Móna recruitment officer that he could maintain machinery. I had seen little evidence of this, though I once watched him repair a puncture on his bicycle. And to his credit, he did teach me how to whittle wood. He could, perhaps, be resourceful when required.

He started work the following Monday and went on to surprise and impress me by building a machine they called a harvester.

It arrived bog-side in bits, on the backs of two low-loader lorries. He and three other men put it together with the help of a small crane. It took them the best part of six weeks.

I'd call down to the edge of the work site to sit and watch my father build. There were moments when the wind whipped tears of pride from my eyes. I'd brag about him to my friend, James Burke.

My father drank less while he worked on the harvester. The harvester put food on the table.

When built, my jaw gaping, I watched him climb up into its metal cab and drive it over the bog.

"The bog surface is ninety percent water, son," he told me. "And I'm steerin' a twenty-two tonne harvester on top of it. I'm not a machine driver at all, I'm a ship's captain."

I wanted to sail the harvester.

I left school the following year, hoping for a job with Bord na Móna. Poor weather meant peat production closed down for the first part of the season. They stopped recruiting. My father stopped driving the harvester. Men were laid off.

A poster went up in the town asking for people to work through the bad weather keeping the drainage ditches open. My mother and father argued. My father applied. He got one of the jobs. That's how he lost his leg.

7

I read the email from Paul McDonnell again and reflected on the implicit sadness, the unfulfilled yearning for a missing mother. *"I've been thinking about her a lot lately."* My book wouldn't provide him with what he needed. I replied and asked him where in Sligo his birth mother lived. Ireland was like a village, someone might know of her.

He emailed me the next day.

> *From: Paul McD*
> *Date: 12 February 1997, 8:14am*
> *Subject: RE: Your book*
>
> *Assuming she hasn't moved, my birth mum grew up and lives in Sligo town, near the coast. There's a long story behind it, which I won't go into now, but I'd like to go back there one day soon. I'd like to meet her, though I realise that's a big step.*
> *I don't know Ireland at all, and I know nobody there. I wouldn't want to go back unless I was with someone who knew the place.*

A week later, I summoned the courage to telephone my sister-in-law in Ireland. Though still wary of her anger towards me, the 'therapy of the familiar' worked, telephone calls became easier. She sounded morose. I struggled to cheer her.

Andrea inherited defective deoxyribonucleic acid. The mutated, degenerate DNA gene had inflicted muscular dystrophy on generations of her family. Her daughter, Niamh, wonderfully free from symptoms, carried out the twenty-four-hour care necessary.

Running out of meaningful conversation, I told Andrea about the emails from Australia. She tried to sound interested, but on hearing the echo of a yawn I realised I was only tiring her. She handed the phone to Niamh. I didn't worry, Niamh was easy to talk to.

Niamh lambasted me. "I'm not a cantankerous, angry little bitch."

"Hello, Niamh," I said.

"If Bridgie is me," she shouted, "you'd better re-write chapter eighteen and print a public apology in the Sligo News. Is it because she's a redhead too? I wouldn't have slapped that fella in the puss, the Lynch character, him a priest an' all. We've a nice priest here."

I could hear Andrea in the background, telling Niamh to stop shouting.

"Nearly threw the bloody book into the fire," Niamh shouted. "How could you write that about me, your favourite niece an' all?"

"Front of the book," I said. "The disclaimer. It says it's a work of fiction."

"But is Bridgie *me*?"

I heard the dull stamp of her foot three hundred miles away. "No," I said.

"Why not?" she screamed.

I laughed down the phone and told her I wouldn't say any more about who the characters were based on. "If they're based on anyone at all," I added for greater discretion. There is a 'Niamh' in the book, but she was way off the mark on her selection. I didn't let her know in case it disappointed her further. I relayed the email story again.

"*Her husband*?" Niamh said. She stopped shouting. "He wrote that in the email? Not 'my father' or 'my daddy'?"

"That's what it said."

"She not with his father, then?"

"Maybe not," I said.

"Separated? There must be a registry office or something in Sligo where he could check birth and marriage records. It didn't happen in Templeboy, anyhow, I know that. There's been no separation in Templeboy since God was a baby. Has he her name?"

"Don't know," I said. "That's all it said in the email."

"Get back in touch with him. Ask if he knows his own mother's name. If it's not Sligo town, could be Enniscrone. Or even Ballina. I could ask around. God, what a scandal. Wait, can you trust him? He wouldn't be making it up, would he?"

"Who knows?" I chuckled into the phone. "Seems genuine enough. How else would he know Sligo?"

"Because you describe it in the book, you eejit." She was right. About me describing it in the book, not, I hoped, about me being an eejit. "The whole world knows about Sligo now," she continued. "And Templeboy."

I did a quick calculation of how many book sales it would take for the whole world to know about Templeboy.

"There's talk of building an airport up the road in Easkey to rival Knock International," she said. "I'm not joking. To cope with all the book-tourists flying in from America and Australia."

A nice thought. "I can imagine you," I said, "driving the tourist bus. 'And this bridge, ladies and gentleman, is where the author used to urinate into the river when caught short on his way home from school.'" I waved an open hand away from me then realised Niamh couldn't see it.

"Tell him come over," she said.

"He knows no-one there."

"You come too, he sort of knows you. Yes, that's it, come over to promote the book. Do some shows or something. Get yourself on Radio West. Stay with us. The two of you. We've plenty room."

Promote the book? On the radio? I could feel my throat constrict. I couldn't shut Niamh up.

"They've run out of *The Harvester* in Scott's Foodstore. I'll tell Peter you'll bring a load over with you. He'll organise a book-signing beside the fridge units, it'll be a laugh. Come on, do it. Please. We haven't seen you in ages. By the way, listen, Mary Gullion's husband is dying. Lung cancer, the poor devil. But sure he smokes like a bog fire, has done for years. It'd be great to see you again. Will you come over?"

8

Mary Gullion. Let me tell you about Mary Gullion.

She was Mary O'Brien when I first met her, and she sat in front of me in Mrs McLinchy's class. All the boys noticed her and would whisper to each other when she passed, talking out of the side of their mouths like horny little gangsters. I admired her neat little arse when she rose to hand out the pencils for Mrs Mac and, over the course of two years, watched it bloom from a boxty-cake flatness into the pear-shaped ripeness of puberty. My thoughts gave rise to sins I could not share with a priest in any confessional.

As our final school year drew to a close I grew worried I'd never see Mary again. I overcame my timidity and asked her if she would walk out with me. She accepted. I was so shocked she said "yes" to the skinny lad with spots I had an uncontrollable nervous outburst of profanity. Mary arched an eyebrow but didn't rescind her acceptance.

We met in secret the next day. We walked. I talked a little; Mary talked a lot. We laughed and flirted in that awkward, childish way. Mary was a good talker. And funny. We met every fourth day. Then every second day and before long, every day. We'd walk a field, or a wood, or alongside a stream. Or we'd climb the hill at the back of her uncle's cabin to the waterfall locals called 'the spout'. Anywhere to be on our own, unseen. We didn't need anyone else.

Mary had good teeth. I mention it because, for most of the children I grew up with, care of teeth had a low priority. Many had lost half a mouthful by the time they were a dozen years old. Teeth that survived the sugar sandwiches and the home-made toffee and the lack of a toothbrush, turned brown from smoking Player's Navy cigarette butts. Mary's mother wouldn't allow her to eat sugar sandwiches, and Mary didn't smoke Player's Navy cigarettes. Although, if she found an empty packet on the street she would cover it with her foot and sing, "Sailor, sailor, bring me luck, find a shilling in the muck." I don't recall the chant ever working. But she did have good teeth.

And hair with gentle curls, almost black, the colour of peat.

I knew it would be a bad idea to let her mother find out that Mary and I were keeping company. Too nervous to ask her father's permission, too terrified to speak to the mother, I took measures to keep it covert. Her mother found out within a week.

That should have meant the end, but Mary encouraged me to call to her house to collect her to go on one of our walks.

When I eventually summoned enough courage to do so her mother surveyed me from the front door with narrow eyes, her head angled forward. She set her body square, like a combatant challenging an aggressor. The words she had for me tended to bluntness and sarcasm. "Seen more condition on a plucked gander. Not off the grass ya licked that, though."

When I challenged Mary about it she laughed it away. "She's fond of you. If she wasn't, she'd split the head of you before you got through the gate."

9

Two days after telephoning Andrea and Niamh I re-opened Paul McDonnell's first email. The seed of a plan germinated in my mind. I wasn't proud of it, not the type of plan you'd boast of, came with challenges and risks and triggered a tremble of fingers over the keyboard, but I didn't care.

I read, "*a single mum in 1958*".

My family emigrated to England in the late fifties.

I asked Paul McDonnell if he knew his birth mother's name.

A response came back.

> *From: Paul McD*
> *Date: 20 February 1997, 7.21am*
> *Subject: RE: Your book*
>
> *Hello. No. I've had people look into it for me and they don't share that sort of information. I have a birth certificate but it's very scant. They'll only send what they call non-identifying information. Chocolate teapot stuff. If I went over, I know I'd find out with a bit of detective work. Local priest would know? Or a public records office? I would like to find her. Not to create trouble. Just to know. Don't want to go on my own, don't know the place. Do you ever go back to Ireland?*
> *I'm enjoying the book, nearly finished it. Learning a lot about the area and its people. Need to schedule in more time for reading, work gets in the way!*

The seed had taken root, and it started to sprout.

10

His new job for Bord na Móna was as banksman, working with a bog-ditcher. My father walked the bank edge, ahead of the ditcher machine, on the lookout for buried stone and bog-wood. The third rainy day into the job he slipped in the sodden peat and tumbled into the ditch. The twelve-foot metal disc attached to the side of the ditcher, rotating at over 124 revolutions a minute, sliced into his leg before the ditcher driver could stop it spinning. My father held on to the leg for a while, but he lost the job immediately.

When buying two slices of ham for my mother in the shop in Easkey I overheard a man tell the shopkeeper that my father was drunk when the accident happened. The shopkeeper said my mother could pay him another time for the ham.

I can still picture the lacerated leg. I won't dwell, but I will mention a deep hole below the knee that my father packed with paraffin gauze dressings to denude the wound of pus and necrotic flesh. Whilst I held the flat tin of dressings aloft he peeled off patches of gauze with tiny tweezers and folded them into the cavity, and I breathed in the sickly-sweet smell of decay. He warned me not to touch the gauze, but I couldn't resist sliding a finger over the slimy greasiness of the petroleum jelly when he had his head down. He had a poorly-stitched, foot-long gash where his calf muscle used to be. James Burke owned a leather football with neater lacing.

Though we had little money coming into the house my father managed to find enough to buy drink. The wound wouldn't heal. He and my mother argued. He went away to the regional hospital. Three weeks later he came back, but left the lower half of his right leg in Castlebar.

I didn't want to leave Templeboy, nestled as it is between the Atlantic Ocean and the Ox Mountains in County Sligo, but my father couldn't work the farm following the accident and he was unable to climb up into the harvester with one-and-a-half legs.

He fashioned himself a wooden stump out of alder, later found to be susceptible to woodworm, attaching a strap that passed over his shoulder to hold it in place. He even shaped a foot on its end to carry a boot. But he never trained himself to dig with it. He enquired after work in England that required minimal mobility.

I, however, still hoped to get work with the Bord on the bog. I longed to steer the herculean harvester. And I had Mary.

Mary O'Brien was, by then, my first love.

Who was it wrote, *The First Cut Is the Deepest*? Whoever it was I know his assertion to be true.

11

In our third pub of the evening, a hundred yards nearer the crossroads at the end of Main Street, Paul slept upright on a bench seat against the wall. His red waterproof was draped beside him. His hair looked darker damp. His knees glistened bronze. Rainwater pooled the floor beneath the coat.

I tried to imagine him at his work. A businessman, business-dressed in suit and tie and flamboyant red braces. It must pay well for him to afford this trip so readily. I smothered a hiccup and wondered what type of organisation employed drunks.

Air rasped in and out of Paul's gaping mouth.

I sat slumped on a highstool by the counter. Though confident with drink I was relieved Paul and I were the only two customers left in the pub on that quiet Sunday night. His full pint sat on the counter beside me, its once creamy head concaved and yellowing. My pint glass was empty. A thin film of whiskey lay in the base of my tumbler. I resented it evaporating into the atmosphere. I drained the glass.

The night was on the tipping point. I'd experienced it many times. Drunk enough to want more drink, to never stop drinking, I was sober enough to think about the next day. I feared my appointment in the morning but took relief from fearing it. There was a time when I wouldn't have given it a second thought.

Why had I got involved in this escapade, helping another drunk search for his mother? What had any of that to do with me? I blamed Niamh for suggesting I come over to Ireland, for mentioning Mary, for planting the seed.

We were due to surprise Niamh and Andrea by turning up unannounced for a two-week visit. Though Niamh had invited

25

me, I never accepted, preferring instead to preserve the perverse family tradition of arriving unexpectedly in a blaze of confused and panicked delight. It now seemed a bad idea. Paul and I. A couple of drunks. Niamh and Andrea had enough to cope with.

We were keeping Fiona, the owner of Pac's Bar, from her bed.

"Are ye working round here?" Fiona asked, stifling a yawn.

"No. I mean, not really," My speech was slow. "We're here to find Paul's mother." As I flicked my head in Paul's direction the latch on the pub door rattled and the door creaked open.

A man in a dirty fawn jacket, a wet stain spreading from the shoulders, shuffled in behind a cold, damp breeze.

Fiona glanced up at the clock and tugged at the ponytail that pulled her blond hair back off her face. She called to the man, "Ah, now, Marcus?"

"Chance of a drink, Fiona?" Marcus said. He staggered but recovered himself. "Please. Just the one, will ya?"

"Marcus, I'm thinkin' you've enough taken already." Her voice was reasonable but forthright. "You'll need to be doin' a one-eighty, good man yourself."

"I'm only in town since nine," Marcus pleaded.

Fiona squeezed words out the side of her mouth. "He must think I rolled out from under a hen's arse this mornin'. Too tired for this." Then louder, "Did you meet up with Eamonn tonight, Marcus?"

"I did."

"And is he well?"

"Well enough."

"He was staggerin' into The Court at about six," Fiona said.

Marcus glanced at me, stared at Paul, nodded to me, and turned back to Fiona. "No. He wasn't. We were in Cleary's."

Fiona smiled. "And you not in town until nine? A one-eighty, please, Marcus." She twirled a slim finger in the air. "You've enough for one night. Head home before that rain gets too heavy on ya. These lads will be finishing up soon."

Marcus shrugged. "Alright, Fiona." He turned to go but changed his mind at the last moment and reached a wavering arm over the counter. "A half, just?"

She shook his hand. "Safe home, now."

"Thank you, Fiona." Marcus shuffled off, back out into the rain, drinkless. "Night, Fiona."

"Never seen such a conciliatory eviction from a pub," I managed to say. "Certainly not in Birmingham, anyway."

Fiona wanted to talk about Paul. "Find his mother, you say? Here in Ballyhaunis?"

"No, up in Sligo."

"Sligo?"

"Yes."

"Not Ballyhaunis?"

I'd told her it was Sligo. "No."

She sighed and nodded. "Right." She furrowed her thin eyebrows. "When you say 'find her', they lose touch, or what?"

"Never had touch, from what he tells me." I gave a drunken smile. Fiona was easy to talk to, especially with drink inside me, but my fuddled mind tried to make sense of her slightly odd behaviour. I wondered would she serve me another whiskey. "He was adopted out of Ireland as a baby," I said. "Young, unmarried mother. Nearly forty years ago."

Her eyes widened. "I'd a feelin' you were goin' to say that." She stared at Paul. "And he's come back to Ireland to find her?"

"All the way from Australia," I said.

"Are you two related?"

"Good God, no."

"So where do you come into all...?" More finger circles.

"He read my book."

The weight of all her questions caused her head to tilt. "And tell me this, does she know he's here?"

"Does who know?"

"The mother." Her tone hinted she had used up her night's reserve of tolerance of drunks.

27

"No."

"Right." Fiona folded her arms. "And don't you think you should've got in touch and told her you were coming?"

"He doesn't know who she is," I said. "He only knows he was born in Sligo. Anyhow, she's probably not even there anymore."

"And what if she is, and you two just land on her doorstep without warning? What about his father?"

I shifted on the highstool. "Disappeared. Thinks she married someone else since."

"And has she other children?"

"We don't know."

"Ye don't know?" She rubbed the middle of her forehead, blinking. "Don't you think ye should have determined all these things before setting off on this mad caper?"

My foot slipped off the crossbar of the barstool. I got a hand to the counter before my face fell against it.

"Go steady!"

I pushed myself up. "I'm fine," I said, regaining composure. "He wants to find his mother. He's entitled to–"

"And what about the mother? Does she not have a say in all this? What about the life she has now? Her husband? Does her husband know about yer man?" Fiona nodded her frowning face at Paul.

"I honestly don't know if–"

"Jesus, ye lads need to think this through before ye get to Sligo." She struggled for a second to contain what she wanted to say, and failed. "What if she *is* married, to a different man, and the husband *doesn't* know about him over there? What d'you call him, Paul is it?"

I folded my arms, pursed my lips, nodded.

"What if his mother is married," Fiona said, tapping the counter with the tip of a finger, "and the husband doesn't know she had a child? How do you think the husband will react when you walk in with *him*?" The finger stopped tapping and pointed at Paul. "Did either of you stop to think what kind of a rat's nest you'd be stirrin' up?"

I considered telling Fiona that I intended putting a call out for the mother during my interview tomorrow, but I didn't want this to be my argument anymore.

"How do you think the *mother* will react?" Fiona continued. "Jesus, why don't men ever think?"

"The mother will want to meet him," I said. "Why wouldn't she? He's her son." The argument was won, no mother would reject her son.

"She might dread it with every fibre of her being."

I thought, at first, I misheard her. I glanced over my shoulder at the sleeping Paul and raised a finger to ask her to repeat what she said. But when I turned back there was a certain set to her eyes, a faraway stare, focused on a place hidden to me.

A shallow crescent of water, that she didn't blink away, built on the lower lid of an eye.

The right and decent thing to do would have been to look away, to leave her to her emotion. But the drunken fledgling writer in me forced me to watch, to observe, to try to understand what emotion predicated this behaviour. I came up with nothing. It made no sense. The urge was to challenge her.

Fiona murmured, "Not an easy dread to carry..." She shook the gaze away and flashed me a momentary glassy smile of apology. Empty pint jugs chinked as she busily moved them from one drip mat to another drip mat. When she finished she rubbed her face, sniffed and looked up. "How old would she be? The mother, how old's the mother?"

"I've no idea."

"How old's yer man?"

"Late-thirties, or something." I wanted to ask where her gaze had been.

Fiona scrutinised Paul, her brow creased. I could see her assessing if late-thirties was a fair and accurate age for the drunk on the bench seat. "Young when she had him. That'd make her our age. Mid to late fifties, am I right?"

"So?"

"So, think on this. Please. She's a woman in her fifties, forced to give up her baby forty years ago. Probably tormented by it every day since. And now he's just goin' to rampage back into her life. A life she's worked hard to establish. And without givin' her any warnin' at all. You comfortable with that?"

"He's her son." I straightened my spine, stuck out my chin. Why did this mean so much to her? "Isn't he entitled?"

"No. No, I don't think he is. Not without the mother's consent." Fiona turned away, took a clean glass from a shelf, stuffed a tea towel into the neck of the glass and twisted. "He's not entitled." The glass squeaked in timid protest. "And if she saw him in that state, think how delighted she'd be." She held the glass up to the light, it still glistened, then returned it to the shelf.

I debated reaching for Paul's yellowing pint but feared the weight of it would topple me off the stool.

"Why now?" she asked.

"Why what now?"

"What's made him want to find his mother now? Why now?"

"Meant to for some time. Told me he's thought about doing it since he reached thirty. Significant year for him, somehow."

"Jesus, I don't know." Fiona threw down the towel. "Just look at the state of him. And short trousers in this weather?"

Paul snored from the bench seat and farted.

I lifted an eyebrow.

Fiona gave a cynical smile and shook her head. "Christ almighty."

12

Mary O'Brien got a new bicycle for her sixteenth birthday. An aunt in Galway sent the money. Her father emptied her uncle's car of the chickens that roosted within and drove her to Sligo town. Mary told me she bought the bike from a shop on Quay Street. She fell off it on Old Quay Court, leaving skin from an elbow on the cobbled stones. When she got the bike home her mother insisted the Parish Priest, Father Brendan Kealey, come and bless it before Mary had another mishap. This he did, drenching it in holy water and asking God to watch over Mary when she went cycling.

The saddle of my father's bicycle came up to the shoulder of my brother, though resourceful little Sean somehow managed to ride it askew. He'd twist a hip and leg in through the gap under the crossbar to reach the pedal on the other side. His contorted little body would bob up and down, propelling himself and the rattly bike along. But with my father convalescing I insisted that I, the eldest son, had first call on his bike.

Mary and I would cycle from Templeboy to Easkey, pausing for breath when we reached the concrete pier crowded with spin fishermen hoping to hook a pollock or a mackerel. As she grew more confident on two wheels we'd push on to Enniscrone. There, we'd drop the bicycles on the sand and walk along the beach. Walking felt less rushed, time slowed from the furious pedalling, we were more connected, and Mary could talk without shouting.

I liked to listen to her talk. She talked of the elements as though they were people. The wind was a bully, pushing us until we did its bidding, another day tender, stroking our backs. Clouds were vexed, frowning because we were so far from home, artists the next day, sculptors of silvery gates in the sky and great stairways to heaven, and, on one occasion, an apron-confined three-breasted bosom of her mother. Childish personifications that, when Mary spoke them, sounded to me like new music.

It was rare for there to be anyone else around. Mary often removed her shoes and left dance steps in the sand.

Enniscrone Beach became our favourite destination. We sometimes shared a half-penny wafer sandwich of ice-cream; the thrill of intimacy as Mary placed her mouth where my mouth had been. More often than not a stiff Atlantic breeze blew in from Killala Bay, whipping sand into our hair. Seagulls, held aloft by draughts, hovered overhead and shrieked at me in disapproval as though some avian sense gave insight to the longing that nestled inside my teenage mind.

When the bullying wind grew too strong, and the sand stung our eyes, we sought shelter behind the clubhouse of the new nine-hole golf course. I don't remember seeing anyone play golf on the manicured surface that year. My father often claimed that very few local men had the price of a golf ball, never mind the price of a golf club to hit it with.

Huddled, one summer's afternoon in July, in the lee of the clubhouse gable, Mary said, "Do you think we'll ever get married?"

I swallowed hard and looked out over the forsaken fairway. A seagull landed near a bunker, tidied its black-tipped wings, and waddled sideways towards the finely-cut grass of the green.

"Would you be let marry me?" I said. "Amn't I a bit rough for the likes of you?"

She understood what I referred to. "I'd be marrying *you*, not your daddy. God would understand that."

I said, "I'm more worried about what your father and mother'd think. They mightn't be as understandin' as God?"

"Isn't it up to me whom I marry?" she said.

Mary was fond of using words such as 'whom', words only she and Mrs McLinchy used.

The landed seagull spotted us and glared. No fear.

"No," I said. "It isn't."

Mary walked two fingers through the sandy grass and touched a knuckle of my hand.

I shuddered.

She giggled. "Are you frightened of me?"

"No."

"Then hold my hand."

I wriggled a finger over hers.

She said, "That's not holding–"

I leaned over to kiss her mouth. I kissed her nose, bumping her face with my cheek and causing her to flinch.

The seagull stretched its neck and looked away.

Mary chuckled and raised a hand to her eye. "Ouch."

The sun felt too warm. I wanted the breeze to come around the corner of the clubhouse and take the hot flush away.

"That's not holding my hand, either," she said.

"Can I try again?" I said.

She looked around, took her finger from under mine and pushed her hair back behind an ear. "It's my turn," she said. "*I'll* attempt to kiss *you*."

The seagull turned its back on us and crabbed towards the flagstick.

"I don't mind." I twisted my face to her.

Mary's kiss was perfect, right on my lips and softly puckered. A slight tilt of her head ensured our noses didn't knock together. And she managed it all with her eyes closed.

13

The fatty-sweet aroma of browning bacon met me in the hallway. I stumbled towards the breakfast room, my movement uncertain, my arms and legs too light. My head throbbed. My skin prickled. My kidneys ached. I needed to scratch at my face and neck. I needed to lie back down and close my eyes. I needed another drink. With a flat hand to my mouth I tested my breath: stale beer, whiskey, denture paste.

Paul tapped at the hall window and smiled in. He was on the drive dressed in running shorts and vest, the vest stained dark with sweat at the centre of his chest. Grinning, he pointed to a bulky black watch on his wrist.

"It's nearly time we were heading to the station," I said. I was too loud, but he still couldn't hear me through the double-glazed window.

"Sorry 'bout last night, mate," Paul said sitting down to a bowl of cereal. He picked up an ivory-handled spoon. He seemed perky. Perkier than me. He smelled of fresh air and soap and expensive aftershave. He wore long trousers.

"Feel a proper galah," he said tipping a tablespoon of sugar over his cornflakes. "Not normally such a beer monster."

"What's a ga–?"

"Mrs G, how you goin' today? Who says it always rains in Ireland? It's glorious out there."

Mrs Griffiths entered the breakfast-room-that-had-been-a-lounge, and skirted around the table, smiling at Paul. She adjusted cutlery and condiments. "Someone smells very nice," she said. "You were up and out early this mornin'. Joggin' was

34

it?" She nodded in answer to her own question. "Tea or coffee? And I've done you a full-Irish. Will you be havin' a full-Irish?"

"Tea and full-Irish sounds great, Mrs G. Same as my author friend here. No milk in the tea, please."

Mrs Griffiths jutted a hip against the table, intent on conversation. A tea towel draped a freckled arm, a pen poised over a redundant order-pad in her hand. "Oh, you write books do you?"

Paul filled the gap. "Written one about the peat bogs, Mrs G," he said. "Called *The Harvester*. He's goin' on the radio this mornin'. Sell a few more thousand copies."

"Radio West?" Mrs Griffiths said. "To talk about the book, is it? Who is it yer on with?"

I forced myself to make eye contact. "A Johnny Madden. Do you listen?"

"Johnny's very good," she said. "He's a great show, very busy. Full of old news and interviews. He doesn't hold back, the same Johnny, takes no prisoners, but he's lovely with it. What time did he say you're on?"

"About ten. But I'd like to get there early." I wanted to ask what she meant by 'takes no prisoners'.

Paul chomped his cereal, cheeks bulging.

"He does mornings, alright," she said. "I'll listen out for you. Be sure to give the B and B a mention on air, won't you? 'Twill be good for business."

Paul leaned forward over his bowl, flakes of corn visible in his grin.

"Of course, Mrs Griffiths. I'll try to work that in."

The modernity of the smoked-glass frontage looked a stark contrast to the pastel-painted façades of the buildings that ran up and down the street either side of it. A County Mayo flag hung in the window, the red and green surrounding a shield that made me think of coffin ships and tombstones. Beside it hung a chequered yellow and blue flag of County Roscommon, demonstrative of the split loyalties of a town less than four miles from the county border. A brown plaque on the entrance vestibule wall declared the building Radio West Broadcast Centre.

Paul took photographs of the street. "How about I get a pic of the author beside the plate?" he said, waving me into position.

"Can we not just go in?" I said. "My head's pounding, my mouth's dry, and I'm nervous enough without you making me even more self-conscious."

"We need a picture of the best-selling author, mate. Hold on 'till I get this right."

"Sod off with your 'best selling author'. I've probably sold half a dozen books, two of which you and I bought, and you're acting like I'm Stephen bloody King."

Paul laughed and hid his face behind the bulky black camera. "Smile."

Plaque-picture taken, we went inside.

I forced myself through a stilted conversation with a white-haired priest sitting next to me in the control room. He was friendly, but I took care not to exhale in his direction.

Johnny Madden sat the other side of a large pane of glass, his words coming out of the audio monitor. He sounded confident, stringing whole monologues together without deviation, repetition or hesitation. Great for a radio panel game, I thought.

I tugged at the collar of my shirt and pushed the hair back off my forehead with the back of my hand. I wanted the producer, sat with his back to us, to turn the volume down. I needed a drink. I wanted to vomit. I stood up, and rolled a ten euro note in my pocket into a tight tube whilst I paced the floor.

Paul tried to calm me. "Steady, mate…She'll be right."

But I knew Australians said that no matter how un-right the situation was going to be. And I still wasn't sure I wanted to be his mate.

The producer spun his chair around. "Mr Madden'll go to the news next. When he does, he'll come out for ya. You'll be using the green microphone, it's the only one workin' properly. Y'alright?"

"Yea," I said. "Just looking for my glasses." My mouth smiled. "For my notes."

"Just, ya look a bit pasty and that," the producer said. "Y'nervous?"

"No."

"Everybody is. But there's no need t'be. You can bring yer pal in with ya if that'll help." The producer pointed a thumb at Paul.

Paul gave an exaggerated smile and nodded. He wanted in.

I checked the location of the exit doors, reminded myself that I had come a long way since my meetings with the analyst, and took two deep breaths.

"Here we go," the producer said. "All set to speak to a hundred thousand potential fans?"

Sweat gathered at the base of my spine. My head pounded. I checked my notes but the words on the sheets melded to a blur. I found it difficult to arrest the quiver in my hands.

A musical trailer replaced Madden's voice, followed by the melodic, strident tone of an unseen female newsreader. The voice sounded familiar, but I couldn't put a name to it. I absorbed snippets of news: a trial of someone called Patrick Gillaney for soliciting two men to murder his wife, the trial transferred to Dublin Circuit Criminal Court at the request of one or the other's legal team.

Johnny Madden tugged open the door to his studio and raised a palm to the priest. "Father Chris." To me he said, "You the author?" He was taller than he looked through the glass.

"Hello, Johnny," I said, shaking his hand. "I signed a copy of the book for you."

"*The Harvester*," he read. "Come in and sit by the blue microphone." He turned to his producer. "Can I get a cup of tea?"

I looked to the producer for confirmation of the correct microphone, but he scurried out of the control room to make Johnny Madden's tea. I managed to raise a hand to wipe perspiration from my forehead and strove to form words. My first interview on the radio and my mouth too dry to talk.

Madden glanced over the back cover and discarded the book beside the audio console.

I regained control of my tongue. "Your producer said–"

"Come in, quick, we've little time." Madden ushered me into the tight studio and closed the door before Paul could make it in. "Please sit."

The newsreader finished by telling us there was only one winning ticket in Saturday night's national lottery draw. No-one had yet come forward to claim the prize. With a giggle she told us all to make sure we check our pockets.

The yellow microphone was nearest, to avoid sidling past the crush of chairs, I sat behind it. "I was thinking of mentioning–"

"When this link is over," Madden said, hands working his console, "I'll introduce you and we'll be off." He stared up at a clock.

A male-voice choir sang out the name of the radio station, acapella style.

Madden pressed buttons and pushed slide controls up and down. A red light illuminated above my head.

"I'm joined in the studio today by the author of a book called *The Harvester*." Madden's voice was smooth, professional. "The book is about the peat industry in County Sligo, and it's set in the nineteen-fifties, a difficult and challenging time in our history with the Irish economy languishing in the doldrums." He pointed at me with a shirt-sleeved arm. "Your hands seem a bit too soft for you to know anything at all about the peat industry."

The challenge drained my mouth of moisture. "Well..." My mumble wasn't the reader-recruiting response I had hoped for.

Madden was the only person to hear it. He glared at me and flicked a finger at the blue microphone. "Move!" he mouthed. I couldn't hear him, but I knew he was shouting.

I rushed to gather my papers, fumbling. As I raised myself from the chair my pen slipped off my notes. It bounced and rattled on the desktop and clattered off a tea-stained mug. I lunged to catch the rolling pen before it fell to the floor. My foot tangled in the cable of the green microphone. The microphone dipped towards the ground, bowing me a welcome, and crashed into the arm of a chair. The loud, harsh crackle filled the studio.

Madden lifted his headphones clear of his ears.

I gave a small sideways hop to clear the cable, lost balance and fell backwards onto two chairs. "Fuck!"

The chairs shifted in opposite directions, colliding with other chairs. I sprawled onto my arse between them, jarring a hip on the rigid metal arm of a swivel caster.

Sheets of typed notes, marked with red scribbled annotations, descended around me.

Madden stood up, face rigid, eyes narrow, his cupped hands over the foam cover of his microphone. He opened his mouth to say something then held back. He sat down. "We'll be right back after *Hotel California* by The Eagles." He stabbed at buttons and slides and slapped the black microphone away from his face.

14

One warm evening, late July, the sun setting light to Killala Bay, we kissed with our mouths open. It was awkward at first, teeth chipping together, our mouths rotating like the twin agitators in the new spin washer James Burke's mother bought from the Electricity Supply Board salesman. We pushed, relented, pushed again and strained our mouths as if to swallow each other's faces. We engaged our bodies in the kiss, shoved into each other, fought for dominance, yielded. Mary let out a whimper that pleased me. I thought it manlier to stay quiet. We drew air through our noses. My ears popped. Our lips lost contact, sliding apart in the frantic melee. We giggled, reorientated ourselves and resumed, calmer this time. When Mary kissed my tongue the blood drained from my head and I nearly passed out.

Mary pulled away, maybe because her jaw ached. I was glad of the rest but was overcome by a devastating feeling of loss. She reached a hand towards me, I feared to push me away and maybe get up and leave. Had I done her wrong? She took my wrist and slowly, ever so slowly, raised my hand to her chest.

I heard myself swallow.

After a pause she undid the buttons of her brown blouse and slipped a hand inside the material, nudging my hand away from her. With a twist of her wrist she scooped a breast clear of its covering, shifted slightly and replaced her hand with mine, inside her blouse. She dipped her head and glanced sideways, exposing her long, pale neck. A sultry beauty, her eyes dark and dilated. Her breath came rapid and shallow.

I could make out the firm bud of a nipple pressing my palm. I dared not move. A pulse throbbed in my temple. My eyes welled. I did, I cried. It was the loveliest thing I had ever held.

Mary O'Brien and I made use of the long, warm evenings and visited the clubhouse almost every day for the rest of that July. We'd cycle there directly, forsaking the walk along the beach. God must have approved because he kept the rain away and pointed the sun at us to warm our exposed skin.

One day in early August, our clothing asunder, the groundsman interrupted us whilst he was clipping the deserted fairways with a horse-drawn mower. Unlike God, the groundsman did not approve.

I got a job with Bord na Móna, my first paid work, at sixteen-and-a-half years old. The hot, dry July had firmed up the peat surface of the bog and production had resumed. The job was not operating the harvester, as I had wished, but shovelling stone.

A small, puffy locomotive with the legend L141 on its flank tugged stone-laden wagons deep into the bog on a narrow-gauge rail. When the loco reached the end of the line its wagons were tipped and we'd spread the stone as foundation for the next section of track. I worked until my hands blistered, my back stiffened and the prints were rubbed off my fingertips.

More annoying than the midges was a grisly old ganger man, whom I knew only as Mr Wymbs, shouting words of encouragement at me whenever I was within earshot. "Shift that stone ya lanky streak o' pig's piss." And, "Ya wouldn't shovel shite from a cuckoo clock." I didn't know what a cuckoo clock was.

Mary's Uncle Frank believed he could earn more money working abroad than he could working for Bord na Móna. He left to pick chanterelles on the Scottish island of Arran for the months of August and September.

Uncle Frank lived deep in the mountains, next to a dirt track off a dirt track. He asked Mary's father to watch over the leaky cabin, to light a fire now and again to keep the black mildew on the inside walls in remission. He also feared a neighbour's herd of cows would break through a repaired gap in the fence and shit all around his front door.

Mary looked after the cabin on her father's behalf. I helped, though her father was unaware of my involvement.

In truth it wasn't Mary's father that worried me. He was an easy going man, contemplative. More prone to outbursts of sighs and resigned nods of the head than outbursts of anger and aggression. Not at all like her mother.

I assume Uncle Frank spent those late-summer days ruffling through leaf mould, seeking out clusters of the bright yellow fungus with the velvety funnel perched on a deeply-veined stalk.

Mary and I spent the evenings ruffling through each other's clothing.

15

We passed the turn-off for Ballaghaderreen on the N83, heading for County Sligo, before I could speak. "What just happened?" I said.

Paul stared forward through the windscreen, camera cradled in his lap. "That Johnny Madden doesn't hang about. A busy show. Things goin' on. Lots of guests to get through. Couldn't keep the priest waitin'."

"What just happened?" I repeated as the car glided over the contours of the road. "That was a disaster."

"What do they say about bad publicity? Don't take it personally. The reciprocatin' electric guitar interplay between Don Felder and Joe Walsh just ate into your time slot, that's all."

I glared at the road, not wanting to look at Paul in case he was grinning. The full-Irish breakfast churned in my stomach.

"You think that bastard Madden played an extended version of the record?" Paul said. "You didn't even have time to mention the B an' B."

"Nor your bloody birth mother," I thought.

Paul had been asleep for an hour by the time we reached Ballina, his long flight no doubt taking its toll. The traffic slowed near the railway station. We halted at a red light. The stop woke him.

"I need to look at a graveyard," I said. "For the next book. There's a scene in an old graveyard, I need to look around it."

"No worries, mate," Paul said and stretched his arms. "I need to buy clothes, but can we get something to eat first?"

"Clothes?"

43

"Like to travel light. Little more than shorts and runners in my bag."

We donned our coats and I limped from the superstore car park to the library on Pearse Street. I told Paul to ask for directions to the oldest pub in Ballina that served food.

The accent, and probably the chiselled chin, drew the attention of the two young women behind the counter. "I'd say that'd be Rouses. Would you, Sarah?"

Sarah stamped the date in another book. "It'd be one of them anyhow." She noticed our blank looks. "Look it, it's across the road and up a bit. Green and red front, you won't miss it … I do go in there myself of an evening." She glanced obliquely at Paul. "I'm there tonight."

I took a breath and stepped forward. "Was Rouses here in the eighteen-hundreds?" It was obvious no-one had ever asked that question before. "It's for a book I'm writing," I said by way of explanation.

The women shared a look.

"You'll have to go in and ask," Sarah said. "We wouldn't have that sort of information here, now."

I was aware of the two women giggling as we walked to the door. I heard, "Sarah Ruddy, you're a brazen bitch."

Traffic choked the road. In Rouses I ordered a pint for Paul and a double whiskey for me.

Paul browsed the menu and nodded a 'hello' to a short, thin woman in a fake-fur hat and coat ensemble who stood at the bar.

She cradled an empty half-pint beer glass to her chest, its inches marked by drying rings of froth. "Are ye the Cork lads up for the match?" the woman asked, leaning towards Paul.

"No, we're not Cork lads," Paul said tittering. "We're in town to see a graveyard."

"But ye have red coats on," the woman insisted. "That's not a Cork accent." She turned, confused, to the man sitting on a highstool next to her. "Haven't they red coats on?" she insisted.

The man's large hands were laced over his large stomach. His thick thumbs danced around each other like miniature boxers. "They have, Julie. They've red coats alright." He nodded a tolerant smile at the woman behind the bar pouring our drinks.

Julie stepped forward and lifted herself onto the bar foot-rail. She leaned her furry head in over the counter and turned it sideways. "Don't they look like Cork men in their red coats, Dominic?"

Dominic sat the other side of us. "No," he said, his eyes fixed on his newspaper.

"Well feck you, Dominic Barrett," Julie muttered. "Sittin' there in yer ol' fartin' jacket. As smart an' all as you are." She turned to the woman behind the bar. "Maureen, don't they look like–"

"Julie, don't be worrying about it," Maureen said and placed our drinks on the counter. "Haven't you been told they're not up for a match? Now come down off that before you fall, and don't be bothering yourself." Maureen gifted Julie a warm smile.

Julie seemed placated.

Paul ordered a steak sandwich and a packet of crisps.

Julie sipped from her empty glass, then rocked on her feet holding the glass close, concealed in the faux fur.

The big man on the highstool said, "Was you the author talkin' on the radio this mornin'?"

"Yea, that was him," Paul said. "Well done. Regrettably, he didn't get to say very much."

I could feel heat rise in my cheeks.

"Father Chris was on after ya swore on air," the man said. "Readin' out the death notices and doin' the weekly prayer, ya know? He said ya had trouble with the microphone, alright. Madden didn't stop gettin' phone calls for the next hour. People phoning in and laughin'. T'was funny to listen to, right enough."

"Sorry, how did you know that was me?" I asked.

The man turned his big head towards me, a satisfied smile on his face. "Father Chris said he spoke to ya. Said ya were headin' for Ballina." The fat thumbs continued rotating around each other on top of his belly. "He mentioned the graveyards…Is it for the next book, it is? He said on air he'd pray you're better with words than you are with your colours. Cheeky enough of him, I thought."

My jaw clenched. I could feel the grin on Paul's face. I wanted to punch him in the throat and shove his arm up his back. I'd been trained how to do that in extreme circumstances. I took two breaths. "Maureen, excuse me," I said. "Would you know if this pub was here in the eighteen-hundreds?"

Maureen moved closer and gripped a beer pump. "Why?" She tilted her head.

"Is it for the book?" the big man said. His thumbs stopped rotating.

Julie shuffled closer.

"Yes. Yes, it is. The book is set in–"

"Here, take this with you," Maureen said, handing me a yellowed letterhead.

I fished for my glasses and read aloud. "P. Flanagan, family grocer, wholesale wine and spirit merchant. Established eighteen hundred and sixty-five. Is this the genuine article?"

"Found a load in the attic," Maureen said. "Hold onto it, we've a few left."

"This is marvellous. I'm…This is great. Thank you. Maureen."

"My family's only here a relatively short while," Maureen said. "Forty years or so. The pub was called Flanagan's before that."

"I know a red coat when I see one," Julie said, and she blew her nose into a linen handkerchief.

The newspaper rustled beside us. "For feck sake, woman. There is no match!"

Paul and I drove up the Killala road past St Patrick's Well to the cemetery.

"Over a thousand years ago," I announced.

"What?"

"St Patrick instructed St Olcan to build him a church. 'Drop your axe to the ground and build me a church where it lands'. St Olcan let his axe fall here, in the corner of this cemetery. This, Paul, is the Kilmore Church of St Patrick."

Paul shrugged.

A centuries-old ruin, cloaked green with ivy, marked the cleaved spot. I intended to bury a character from my next book beside the ruin.

"Lonely enough," Paul said.

I scribbled on the last empty page of a wirebound NHS notepad given to me by the head-woman, "Grave blended into anonymity by the daily wipe of shadow from ivied chapel."

"Hey, will I be in the next book?"

"I'm trying to imagine this graveyard a hundred and thirty years ago," I said.

"They'd be no empty Cidona bottles, for sure."

We drove back into town, crossed the River Moy and took the more scenic Quay Road, alongside the river's channel, towards Enniscrone in County Sligo. The tree-lined route, full of narrow bends, afforded us glimpses of the water to our left. The land and weather seemed to soften as we crossed the county border from Mayo.

We passed bungalows set to the rear of vast lush lawns, their ornate façades bordering on an ostentatious display of self-betterment. Brick-built walls, with elaborate wrought ironwork and animal-bust stoneware, enclosed ornamental gardens with needlessly-narrow entrances. Unlike the English the Irish preferred their gardens to the front.

In other plots grey-block skeletons of sprawling new houses awaited completion. Blue and black and yellow plastic service pipes grew up out of the ground around them. The sites looked abandoned but perhaps only awaited the economic boom to be officially declared before the roofs went on and the windows were installed.

We drove beneath 'For Sale' signs, sticking out over the road, nailed to crumbling stables that threatened to collapse onto the car. Posters pinned on poles told us of country dances taking place all over County Sligo.

The sun came out and dappled the road in tree shadows.

Views of the river became rare as we veered inland. Paul swapped lenses and snapped at the receding glimpses of water. I wondered how pictures from within a moving car would come out.

"You're a keen photographer," I said.

"My brother bought me this for the trip. Expensive. Not too sure how to bloody use it, though."

I shook my head.

We caught a last sight of the estuary and turned left into Enniscrone.

Boards in roadside fields advertised the hotels, bars, and shops we were about to encounter. Seagulls swooped the car, wingtips raked, snowy silhouettes against a patch of azure sky.

A sign for the golf course pointed down a road that divided a building site, a development of identical square houses. I fought off a temptation to turn the car and continued forward through the town along Main Street.

High-spirited holidaymakers, towels tucked under arms, ambled towards Enniscrone Beach. Mid-day drinkers, enjoying the novelty of sitting outdoors in the sunshine, had drinks delivered on trays to bench tables. Men, parked awkwardly on pavements, gossiped out of car windows.

I searched the faces of the women, but I didn't see Mary. "Not far now," I said.

Paul stirred his long frame.

16

The first time. Everyone remembers the first time. The presence of mooing cows, ripping grass from the path verge and shitting over the yard, could not counter the inexorable stampede of hormonal youthfulness. Uncle Frank's cabin. One dry August evening.

Mary's mother and father were visiting an aunt in Tuam in County Galway. I told my mother and father I was staying at James Burke's house.

I don't think we intended it to happen. It started off as it usually did, kissing and fumbling, but something about the darkening evening made it grown up. We paused.

I was ready. Mary was ready. Our bodies told us. I shivered in nervous expectation. Laughter. Silence. Both frightened. The fear failed to stop us.

We overcame the initial clumsiness and discomfort with gasps and winces. We halted, moved apart, and stared at each other with wide eyes, amazed at what we just did. Our breaths rushed, chests heaving. We laced our fingers and came back together.

Re-joined, pain forgotten, we took to it quickly. Our muscles trembled, our cheeks damp from streamed tears. All speech choked back, redundant.

It might sound old-fashioned to say Mary and I 'made love', but on that August night, the room lit by the flicker of the fire in the hearth, every time our bodies locked together, that is exactly what happened: we made love. From basic elements of affection and attraction, friendship, deference and desire, lust and tenderness, we made love.

We made it on Uncle Frank's damp cast-iron spring bed, disregardful of the musty spores of mold our arrhythmic heaving stirred up around us. We made it balanced like acrobats on a narrow pale-blue wooden bench seat, which knocked a beat on the flagstones as it rocked under us. We even made it within the confines of the two-foot-deep windowsill, listening to the dull roar of the spout cascading its crystal waters down the mountain.

I was young and strong, Mary was young and full of imagination. We had no sleep and nothing to eat. And the naked, binding love we made that humid, turf-lit night, out of our own blissful entwinement, stayed in me.

During covert visits to the cabin over the following weeks we sat and planned. A place as small as Uncle Frank's would be sufficient, though we wanted the electricity in. We talked about children. I wanted a girl; she wanted four boys. We'd need to build on. We spoke about 'making it official'. I gave Mary one of a pair of rings I whittled from the branch of a hazel tree. We set a date for the following June, but I talked Mary into keeping it our secret until I herded sufficient courage to confront her mother. Most evenings we sat and said nothing, our arms clasped around each other, listening to the hum, crackle and hiss of burning turf, the dancing flames holding the damp in the walls at bay and drying our eyes.

Uncle Frank returned home at the beginning of October. When Uncle Frank came back, Mary went away.

17

A mile the other side of Enniscrone I turned the car down a narrow, pot-holed lane towards Corballa. I wanted to avoid St Patrick's cemetery but didn't bother explaining that to Paul. A tractor with a flat-bed trailer bearing three young children and a dog had to pull to the side of the track to let us pass.

Paul glanced at me, a hand on the dash to steady himself, as if to ask if I knew where I was going.

The Ox Mountains hung onto the horizon, the contours of their highlands and valleys as familiar to me as the peaks and troughs of my own signature. I knew where I was going.

On the N59 we came alongside the site of the former Bord na Móna works, its peat fields camouflaged in deep heather that bridged the mouths of the drainage ditches like unruly moustaches.

"Used to work out there a long time ago," I said. "My father did too. That's where *The Harvester* is set."

Paul leaned sideways in his seat to capture a picture of the abandoned bog. "None of these'll be right," he said pressing random buttons on his camera.

"It's the author!" Niamh screamed. "Why the hell didn't you say you were coming over?" She flung her arms around my neck. "You've been away so long I'm surprised you were able to find us on your own. God, I thought I was fat but look at you, you're nearly as bad." She patted my paunch.

"Good to see you, Niamh," I said. "How's your mother?"

"Grand enough. You'll see."

"She still angry with me?"

"She's over it. Don't worry." Niamh kissed my cheek. "And who's this? This isn't the fella from the email, is it?"

"This is Paul," I said.

"From bloody Australia?!" she yelled. "Welcome to Templeboy, Paul."

"Hello–" The hug from Niamh swaddled anything else Paul might have said. He smiled over her head with wide eyes.

"There's no excess meat on you is there, Paul?" Niamh said releasing him.

"I'm very bad at triathlon," Paul said.

"Mmm. Come in, come in, come in, both of ye." She led us up a concrete ramp to the house. "Nice car. Ya must be selling a few books."

"It's not mine," I said. "It's Paul's."

"From bloody Australia?" Niamh laughed. "And with Mayo plates."

A calico cat, a highwayman's mask of black across its orange face, sat beneath a window and watched us pass with unblinking eyes, pupils a vertical slit. A wren lay rigid under a white paw.

I dropped my luggage beside the telephone table. "I nearly didn't recognise the house. Almost drove past it."

"That's shameful," Niamh said.

"You've done so much to it," I said innocently. "There were no cherry-blossom trees in the yard in my day. Nor a porch. And is that another room you've had built on?"

"Daddy did the work. He built loads of rooms on. We've barely the money to heat them all. This is Mammy's room for resting." She pushed open a door I didn't recollect. "Mammy, look who's here to see you?"

Andrea sat dressed in a blue and yellow flowered blouse. White slacks covered her leaning legs. Her eyes flicked from me to Paul and back. Her head was tilted a little, back and to the side. The cords in her neck strained to keep it still. A thin, pale arm lay along the armrest. Her long fingers, the nails a glossy coral varnish, contorted around a joystick control. She appeared twisted, the headrest unable to hold her posture straight. The afternoon sun spotlighted her through the window. She smiled. Her teeth were good, her makeup perfect, her cheeks hollow. "Welcome home," she said.

I drew in a deep breath of relief. The house smelled and tasted like home. My shoulders slackened. Jumbled memories of the place fell over me. I thought of my mother, sitting at the kitchen table, the perpetual look of worry, auburn hair falling around her face like a shroud. Of my father, supporting himself on the back of a chair as he knelt into his cap and slurred his way through the six o'clock Angelus prayer. He and his friends then settling down to poitín and tea and a game of cards. I remembered Sean, seven years old, eyes clamped closed, hands pressed in prayer, miming the words to the rosary. I gazed down at Andrea, my brother's wife, and wiped my eyes. "Thank you, it's good to be here." I bent to kiss her.

Andrea stiffened. "They say unexpected guests are a gift from God. Typical of you to just turn up unannounced. Who is this young man?"

"Andrea, Paul. Paul, this is my sister-in-law, Andrea."

"Welcome to Templeboy, Paul."

Paul eased his tall frame forward and offered his hand. "Delighted to meet you, Andrea. Lovely home you have here, in a lovely part of the world."

Andrea reached with her left and clasped Paul's hand. "You're the Australian." She stared up into his eyes. She held onto him, her fingers burrowing deep into his, feeling him.

Paul stared back, not moving.

Niamh, an arm resting on the back of her mother's chair, smiled at me. "You'll both have tea," she said, breaking the moment.

"You must be starving," Andrea said. She let go Paul's hand. "We'll go out to the kitchen. Niamh, the kettle, please. Then make up the beds, good girl." Andrea rocked as the oversized electric wheelchair whirred into motion.

18

I truly believed that Mary was my gift from God. But God got a message to her that He wanted her back. A vocational re-calling. I heard nothing of it from Mary.

Her mother broke the news to me in curt and pithy snippets. From the front edge of her doorstep she leaned forward into her fight stance and spoke her high-pitched jabs and uppercuts. "She's gone. With the father. The uncle took them. Ya won't see her again." Her face was mottled with the strain, but I heard relish in her harsh tone.

A knot tightened in my stomach. "I'll see her when she's back," I said.

"You're not listenin', ya thick," she barked. "She won't be back."

"I don't under– Where's Mary gone?"

Her voice softened. There was a glassiness to her squinting eyes that I couldn't figure out. She groped behind her for the door. "Dublin. She's gone to Dublin. The Blessed Holy Sisters of Mercy. All I'm sayin'."

A nun? I scoffed. "'Course she'll be back."

She roared, "Will ya listen." The fight stance returned. She faced me full on, legs planted wide, bending towards me. "She's gone from us, d'ya hear me? My Mary's gone." Spittle from her mouth flecked the dry stones at my feet. I could smell stale tea on her breath. Her eyes flickered and she lowered her voice. "A callin' from God. Be it known that's what it is."

My head shook. "Why've ya done this?"

Her nostrils flared as she straightened, the blood boiling red in her face. She spat her words at me. "The curse o' Jesus on you and your father." She gasped and gripped the doorframe for support, her fingers gnarled, her knuckles white.

"My father?" I stared, slack-jawed.

Mary's mother glared over my head and struggled to calm herself with controlled breaths. "There's been a vocation in the family," she said. "A divine callin' from God. And Mary is happy." It sounded as if she was reading from a signpost stuck in the field behind me, the words not her own. "We're to thank God for the blessin' bestowed on this house."

I heard her choke back a sob.

"If you're worth anythin', you'd be happy also." She wiped an eye with a wrist and shuffled backwards into the house. She paused to dip a middle finger into a Child of Prague holy water font hooked on the doorframe. The infant Jesus held aloft his cross-bearing orb, his right hand raised in a calming, two-finger posture. Mary's mother blessed herself, took a last look at me, and slammed out the door.

I returned the following evening, immediately after work. I dried my cheeks with a sleeve of my jacket while I waited for Mary's mother to answer my knock.

"Mrs O'Brien," I said to the closed door. "It's me." I shuffled my feet on the gravel, waiting, sobbing.

No response.

"Please tell me Mary's comin' back." My arms jerked at my side. "Tell me what ya said isn't right." I inched closer to the door. "Don't do this. Please don't do this."

Still no response.

I clenched my fists and leaned my head against a blue-painted door plank, the evening condensation cold on my brow. I shouted, "It's you doin' this to Mary, not God. My family, ya hate us. Not good enough. Not good enough for the likes of ye. Well you're wrong." I punched the door. "You're wrong I'm tellin' ya. Please don't do–"

I jerked back when the door opened.

Mary's mother glared out from the gloom, her eyes bloodshot, the rims inflamed.

"Tell me it's not true," I squeaked.

"You need to thank God He had a holy refuge for her." She picked her words with care. "She's followin' her vocation. She's happy now. One of the Holy Sisters."

I couldn't breathe. "No." I gasped. "That's not right … It can't be right." I collapsed to my knees in front of her. Tears came, wetting the dust on my calloused hands as I covered my face and wept. I wailed, "Why didn't Mary tell me?"

"Be off with you. Back to your father. And don't return. There's nothin' here anymore for your kind."

My kind?

"I'll summon the guards and have ya arrested if ya darken our door again."

The door closed out.

I leapt to my feet, tugged the ring off my finger and threw it to the gravel. It bounced against the door, ricocheted off several small stones and came to rest on its edge, determined not to topple.

My rushing breath dried my throat. I clenched my fists tight, my arms taught and strong from working with the shovel. I wanted to hurt someone, break something. I stared over the house.

She was at the window, watching, curious.

I raised a foot and brought it down on the ring, shattering it into tiny shards of wood. I glared at Mary's mother, defiant.

Three years later, a disjointed but welcomed letter from James Burke told me Mary had left the sisterhood and returned to Templeboy. But I had long emigrated to Coventry in England by then, with my brother, my mother and my invalid alcoholic father.

19

My father rushed the move. We left Templeboy before he sold the small farm. Few farmers had any interest in buying the neglected plot.

I remember the local newspaper, *The Coventry Evening Telegraph*, the weekend we arrived in England. A footballer called Mick Kearns finished a Saturday-morning shift at the Massey Ferguson tractor factory and made his professional debut for the local football team at their Highfield Road ground that same afternoon, scoring a hattrick. The newspaper carried a smiling picture of Mick, beside a solemn picture of the city's Whitley Hospital: a ward full of children encased in iron lungs from an outbreak of polio.

Without a trace of irony my father informed us, the newspaper held low at arm's length and reading with his chin raised, that Coventry had been declared the English city with the highest standard of living outside of the south east of England.

My father held down a permanent job in the paint shop of the local Carbodies factory, applying the primer coat to hackney taxis. "You can have one in any colour you want, lads," he'd tell us, "As long as it's black." I thought that was brilliant. It was years later before I learned he had read it somewhere.

In England I attended college and then went on to university. Three years later I stumbled into the wrong room during the graduate recruitment fair they called The Milkround and ended up joining Her Majesty's Prison Service. A jailer.

My brother Sean's destiny appeared to be a choice between following my father into the car factory, and joining the scores of other Irish that drove the double-decker buses around

Coventry's partially-completed ring road. Neither option appealed, so he returned to Templeboy and married a local girl we knew as Andrea McCabe.

Though older than Sean by ten years, more than half his age again, Andrea McCabe was beautiful and intelligent. I remembered her from school. I thought Sean fortunate.

The age difference raised eyebrows, my mother even had concerns about fertility, though most people in Templeboy thought it an act of gentle benevolence by Sean. Andrea was a widowed mother, her husband consumed by tuberculosis a year after Niamh was born.

"If you love each other," my father told him, "then marry. Don't let anyone talk you out of it."

Sean cried when he relayed the conversation to me.

Andrea and Sean bought my father's old family plot and ran it as a working farm. They did well, putting in the effort my father was reluctant or unable to, and made the farm a success. To my mother's relief they gave Niamh a sister, and raised two precocious, delightful daughters.

20

"So that's Paul?" Andrea said.

We were alone, back in the new front room, the transforming sun a ruby glow through the vertical blinds. Paul and Niamh were on a tour of the back yard and outbuildings.

"Seems alright," I said. "His constant grinning grates a bit. And he's a bit fond of his drink, but that's modern businessmen for you."

Andrea's eyes turned to me.

"But who am I to talk?" I admitted.

"How are you doing?" she said.

I knew what was coming. Fearless Andrea.

"Are you managing to stay off it?"

"I'm managing to control it," I said.

Her hand jerked, and the wheelchair spun around to face me.

"That's not the same thing," she snapped.

"I'm fine ... I'm grand ... I had a few with Paul last night, when we met."

"A few? Still incapable of meeting new people without a drink inside you?" Her glare bore into me. She had no smile.

The barb of her words stuck me. "Andrea, that's not–"

"Explains the eyes all yellow," she said.

I turned to the window, blinking. "I can control it."

"Why didn't you *control* it when we wanted you here?"

"Andrea–"

"Your own brother. You couldn't come over for Sean."

"It's not that I–"

She hadn't finished. "His big brother. Going on to be a big detective and all."

"I wasn't a detective," I said. "It was the prison service."

"Forever working you into conversations, mentioning you to who'd ever listen. 'A top detective putting English thugs behind bars'. He was so proud of you, despite everything."

"Alright," I said. "It just wasn't an easy time … I'm sorry." I gazed out at the saffron sky.

"It's too late for sorrys," she said. "You should have coped better with that mishap at work. Drink is a bloody selfish solution."

I could have got angry at her dismissal of what happened to me at work as a mere 'mishap'. I didn't. "It had a hold."

"Has," she corrected.

"Alright, has a hold. I was bad when it happened. Then hearing the news … A random accident like that."

"A *drunken-driver* accident." Another barb? "Nothing random about it."

"Anyhow," I said. "I couldn't handle it. Couldn't cope. Didn't know how to cope. Even the head-woman, sorry, my analyst, thought a booze-laden trip to Ireland a bad idea."

"But locking yourself in a room and drowning your sorrows in a sea of spirits was a good idea?"

I thought back to an early appointment with the head-woman. She pushed her pen into the coiled wire of a new National Health Service notepad and told me, "Your addiction is a misguided attempt at self-medication."

"I don't touch whiskey anymore," I said.

Andrea let the lie pass, said nothing, just stared through me. Like the head-woman Andrea knew it wasn't her I had to convince.

A heat gathered in my neck and ears. "Who was it with Sean on the motorbike?" I didn't want to talk about me. "Was it Laynihan? Wasn't he in our class at school? Sat beside you, near the window?"

"Pat Layden," Andrea said. "It was Pat Layden's bike. Sean was riding pillion … His first time on a motorcycle."

"I'll visit Sean."

Andrea stared into my eyes, her focus flickering from one to the other, searching. "What are you doing here?"

I caught my breath. "What?"

"Templeboy. What are you doing coming back to Templeboy?" She noticed my eyes widen. "Don't look so dismayed, just tell me why you're here. I want to hear it from your own mouth."

"Andrea?"

"In your own words."

We held a stare. I hoped she'd speak first. She didn't. Why had I come back?

"I've the book to promote," I said.

"Oh, yes, the book. So you're here to promote the book? Templeboy's own teller of lies." A mocking tone this time. "We heard you on the radio." A gentle mock, surely? She wasn't cruel.

My hip still ached from the fall.

"What else? What else are you here for?"

I turned back to the window. Red sky at night, traveller's delight. The sun had dipped behind the horizon but its blush reflected off the underside of the high wisps of curling clouds. A sienna-red sea in the sky. I envied the hiding sun. "To help Paul find his mother," I said. "And there's Sean." It came out sounding like a suggestion, a just-remembered afterthought.

Andrea shook her head, belittling eyes locked onto me. "I want to tell you, I'm uneasy about this Paul situation."

"You and Fiona."

"Who?"

"A woman in Ballyhaunis. Look, he asked me to help, I said I would. This is a big trip for him, he's come a long way to do this. It's important to the lad. I mean man."

"Did you ever pause to consider the mother?" she asked.

"I know, I know … I know what you're going to say. No, is the honest answer. Are you happy? No, we didn't fully consider the mother."

She couldn't face me any longer. With a spasm that started in her shoulder her hand rocked the joystick control and her chair turned back to the sunset. She looked aflame in the redness. "I'm sure you'll visit Sean," she said, "but I know you're not here for Paul. You've no concern for him or the mother you seek, have you? You're your father's son … I thanked God the drink and the selfishness steered clear of Sean. The village was delighted it was Sean who returned from England instead of you. Or even worse, your father."

"Hold on, Andrea–"

"What is it you're after? Tell me."

"How do you mean?" I opened out my hands, nothing to hide.

"You haven't told me the full story, have you?" She gave me time to reply.

I didn't reply.

"You haven't mentioned Mary Gullion?" She said it as a question.

I wrung my hands. "Andrea, I know you're friends–"

"The best of friends." Her knees twitched involuntarily. "She's my dearest friend, my oldest friend. And you mustn't hurt her." Her hand grasped the joystick. "I warned Mary you might come."

"Warned?"

"Have you forgotten what happened at the wedding?"

21

It was Niamh, radiant and all self-important in her glistening-silver chief bridesmaid dress, a look of mischief in her brown eyes, who re-introduced me to Mary at the wedding.

I hadn't seen Mary for thirty-four years, but she needed no re-introduction. I adjudged my two failed marriages, and career in an occupation that regularly topped 'the most stressful jobs in the world' league tables, accounted for the difference in how well we carried the years.

Niamh excused herself to watch her sister's new husband perform an unrehearsed karaoke routine to *Everything I Do, I Do It for You*. "He's never sung it before in his life," she said and swished away.

Mary spoke first. "I wouldn't have recognised you."

I thought she was lying but said, "Probably because of the extra poundage I carry around my girth."

"The extra weight suits you." She looked away. "You used to be rake thin."

"Sign of a contented man," I said.

She smiled. "You still in Coventry?"

"Birmingham. Moved about ten years ago. Work."

"I see ... Isn't it prison– Here he is." She turned and smiled at a stocky man staggering towards us in an expensive suit. I shifted to avoid him crashing into me. Mary introduced me to her husband, Joe, from County Kilkenny. Joe Gullion. Mary and Joseph. I wondered if there was a 'Jesus'.

Joe seemed a solid enough man. He took an elaborate step back and swung his arm in for the handshake. Our hands slapped when they made contact. He almost bowed, the front of his unbuttoned jacket flaring. He crushed my hand with thick, nicotine stained fingers and pulled me towards him. A muscle jumped in his neck. The shank of his sovereign ring dug into my finger, and three chain-link gold bracelets slid from under the cuff of his shirt. I felt the weight of their impact on his thumb. He forced a smile, and staggered when he released me.

I congratulated him.

He thought I meant the hurling match being shown on the television in the Seaview Bar. "The result was never in doubt, man. We've it sewn up already." Then he shouted. "M'on the Cats."

Elderly wedding guests, sat in the hotel reception area in refuge from the loud music, glanced over, on edge.

I forced a chuckle.

"D'you follow the hurlin' in England?" Joe asked me.

"Not at all," I said.

He sniffed and swayed his head backwards, appraising me.

Sweat formed on my palms.

In the wedding reception room the groom informed the bride, in amplified song, that he was prepared to die for her.

"Do *you* follow hurlin', Mary?" Joe asked, his tone sarcastic, his eyes fixed on me.

"You know I don't, Joe. Take it easy."

Joe snorted. "I'm goin' back to the match, Mary."

A Kilkenny man to the last, I thought.

"But that's not all I'll be watchin'." The side of his mouth curled before he turned and meandered back to the Seaview Bar.

I felt a disconcerting pull in my gut, and I wished with all my heart that I was him.

"I'm sorry," Mary said.

"What did he mean by–?"

"Are you with anyone?" she asked, staring up at me.

My turn to snort. I told her about the failed marriages. She acted shocked and sympathetic, but something in her face told me she already knew.

She asked about children.

"No," I told her. "Managed to avoid that."

She placed her red lips around the black straw of her drink and paused. She was waiting for me to ask her the same question.

I wanted to ask her about Dublin and the Sisters of Mercy. Why did she go? Why did she leave Templeboy? Why did she leave me?

"I can't have children," she said, looking away again. "We did all the expensive tests, cost Joe a fortune, but they couldn't figure out what was wrong." She sighed and said, "I regret to say, it's all a bit too bloody late now."

There was no Jesus.

Our conversation came to an awkward halt. Mary must have wanted us to work through the barrier because she offered to buy me a drink.

"I'm on orange juice," I said. "And I've probably had enough of the stuff to last me the rest of my life." I held up my glass. "A pharmaceutical company could probably harvest vitamin C from my body."

Cheers, whistles and clapping came from the main reception room, the groom concluding his performance.

"Have a pint of Guinness," she said, a warm smile, her fingertips glancing my arm. "It tastes better in Ireland than it does in Birmingham."

"I'm a recovering alcoholic, Mary. Guinness led me by the hand to the spirits and the spirits to a dark place. I've definitely drunk enough of that to last me the rest of my life."

Her eyes widened. "I do apologise." She took a half-step towards me. "I did know, and I'm sorry." Her fingers tugged at the sleeve of my jacket. "Do alcoholics ever recover?"

"It's why I use the present tense. Still working on it."

She had the nerve to suggest a link between my alcoholism and the failed marriages when she said, "Can be hard being married to a drunk."

"I'm not a–"

A roar went up in the Seaview Bar. Joe. Victory to Kilkenny.

I told her she was right, because she was. "True enough, Mary."

A moment later, Joe rushed over carrying three tumblers of whiskey. He raised the tumblers into the air. "The Kilkenny Cats. A little celebration."

"Ah, Joe." Mary lifted her glass. "I've this. And you know I don't drink that stuff. Have mine, you, though I'm thinking you might've had enough already."

"Drink the bloody whiskey, Mary," Joe said. "We're celebratin'."

Mary's cheeks flushed. She shuffled from one foot to the other. "Joe, don't–"

Joe dangled a glass between thumb and middle finger in front of my face. He swirled the generous measure of amber fluid around the fat bulge of the tumbler's base. Light danced in the liquid's interior.

"Cheers, Joe," I said.

Mary grimaced and cocked her head in question. "You don't have to–"

"It's grand," I said. "It's just the one. With Joe. To the Cats."

"See, Mary. Not everyone's as stuck-up-the-hole as you." He tried to laugh the edge off the remark, rocking himself forward and grinning into my face. The tip of his blue silk tie flirted with the rim of my glass.

Mary glared at Joe. Embarrassment or anger, or both, forbid her to look at me. She flushed crimson. The ice in her drink chinked as she turned and stalked away.

An aching loss welled in my chest as she left, dragging my heart after her as though it was snagged on the slide of the zipper that curved a path down the back of her navy dress.

Joe watched her go, a tumbler of whiskey in each hand. "Fancy a real drink?" he asked without turning. Tiny flakes of dead skin flecked the back of his jacket collar.

"Why not?" I answered.

22

"He can swim like a bloody dolphin," Niamh said.

"Triathlons," I said. "He told you that. Swimming's easy if you do triathlons."

"He also said he was rubbish at it, the liar. And it was getting rough out there."

"An Aussie thing," I said. "A false-yet-endearing modesty."

"Did you not join him, Niamh?" Andrea asked. "An early morning dip in the sea?"

"Full of tricks like that, Mother. Freeze the bloody tits off meself."

"Niamh, enough."

Niamh winked. "I'm taking him into Sligo," she said. "To the council office. I phoned this morning. We'll start the search for his mother there. It's on Riverside is it, Mammy?"

"County Hall, yes," Andrea said. "But I'm not sure what they'll be able to tell you."

"They might tell us where to look next, I was thinking. Point Paul in the right direction."

"What direction is that?" Paul said, entering the kitchen, rubbing his head with a towel. His face glowed hot and glossy, his eyes bright, the lashes thick and long and moist.

"Paul, eat something before you go," Andrea said. "There's sausage and rashers. Help yourself to bread. Niamh, more tea."

I said, "We hear you're heading into the County Hall in Sligo town."

"That's right." His damp hair was dark and ruffled. He looked boyish. "Niamh said she'd take me in. Seems a good place to start. 'Course you're still welcome to come along if you want."

I answered with a you-didn't-mean-that smile. "You and Niamh carry on. If you want, you can update me when you're back."

"Right, Flipper," Niamh said. "No time for tea. Put a few slices of that bacon in some bread and we'll be off."

"Flipper?" Paul said, grinning around the table.

"Traffic's atrocious in Sligo," Niamh said. "And we'll get no sense out of them office workers after their two-hour lunch break in Flannelley's Bar. Best we go now."

Paul loaded up two slices of bread.

"Paul," I said.

He paused and turned.

"Good luck."

"Yea." He gave a pensive sigh. "Yea, cheers, mate."

"I detest this journey in," Niamh said as they left the kitchen. "If that wind wasn't building, *you'd* probably get there quicker swimming around the coastline."

Paul's answer was lost to the rear yard. The back door clicked shut.

Andrea frowned after them. "Don't say a word," she said. "Not a bloody word."

I picked bacon rind from my teeth. "What're you up to today?" I asked.

"Me? Never mind me. What're you going to do with yourself?"

"It was planned that I spend the day with Paul, searching for his mother, but it looks like Paul has been appropriated by my niece."

"Is he not married?" Andrea worked herself forward in her wheelchair, her brow furrowed, her eyes intense with the effort.

"Divorced, apparently. No children, before you ask."

She fell back in her seat.

"Don't you think that's bloody convenient?" I said, laughing. "Now, how do you fancy a drive out?"

68

23

Joe's legs buckled. He caught the counter before he fell and laughed. A tail of ash dropped from his cigarette. The agitated clink of the heavy jewellery around his wrist reminded me of the rattle of jailer cell keys. We were in an empty, airless bar of the hotel, away from the wedding crowd. The pulse of disco music pushed in through the double doors and vibrated the floor beneath us. The carpet was sticky in patches and smelled of spilt beer and tobacco. Pictures of links golf courses from around Ireland adorned the windowless walls. We spoke of hurling, about which I knew little, whilst I thought of Mary. Of Mary and Joseph.

Niamh glanced through the doorway now and again to check on us, one time her brow wrinkled, another time her bottom lip pinched between her teeth. She didn't join us. I estimated Joe and I managed at least a couple of whiskeys to each of her inspections.

The curly-haired barman breathed into another narrow champagne flute before winding a blue and white towel into it.

"How d'ya know Mary?" Joe asked, his voice slurred. He sucked on the cigarette and squinted through the smoke.

"Oh, my God." I shook my head, blowing out through pursed lips. "It's been all my life. I've known Mary all my life. Since school days."

"Hard to believe the daft bitch of a woman ever went to school." He grinned, the crevices between his teeth smoke-stain brown.

I glanced at Curly Hair, who paused the polishing.

"She was in charge of the pencils," I said forcing a smile. "And she was the best scholar in the class."

"I bet you thought she was," he said and turned to lean his back against the counter. He folded his arms over the bulge of his belly, crumpling his jacket and tie. Smoke curled up between us from his fingers. He frowned and glared at me with baleful eyes. "I know who you are."

I shook my head at him and drained my glass. I needed to loosen my tie.

"What do you earn as a drunk detective?"

"I'm a prison officer. High Security. Birmingham. Not a detective."

"A drunk prison officer?" He scoffed. "Probably on less than a detective."

"I wouldn't know."

"Listen to me." He leaned closer. "I can see the way. Way she looks at you. Thinks I'm fuckin' stupid. The mother put me straight on Mary, she told me what went on. Her mother told me everything ... I know you." He waited for me to respond, to explain, to confess.

I said nothing.

"Keep the fuck away from her," he said and thrust his jaw out into the smoke. "You were no good to her then and you're useless to her now."

Curly Hair moved a discreet distance away from us.

I creased my brow. My arms opened out in a shrug and flopped back to my side.

Joe said, "She might be a fuckin' whore, but now she's *my* fuckin' whore."

I clenched a fist and aimed a punch at his chin.

24

We watched the sea churn. The black seven-segment writing on the silvery display told us the radio was tuned to 'Radio West: Johnny Madden'. The volume was turned too low to hear the words coming through the speakers.

The car rocked against the Atlantic gusts.

"One of the twenty castles of O'Dowd," Andrea said.

The ocean devoured Easkey pier in a great swallowing wave. No fisherman would have braved dangling a line in this weather. Nor were there a pair of bicycles propped against the pier wall, one old, one new, with two nervous teenagers together but pretending not to be.

Becalmed waves ran in along the rocks, dissipating on the bouldered splash apron. Breakers fell into foam on the sand ahead of us. To our right we could make out the Benbulben Mountains, black and ghostly shadows, through the sea mist.

"I know that," I said. "I went to school around here too."

"Alright, smart arse, which one of the twenty is it?"

"Eleven."

"No, it's not," she said.

"Twelve."

"It's number ten. Eleven's at Dromore. Twelve's somewhere else."

"You're wrong. This is number eleven. Dromore's twelve."

"This is ten. Always has been and always will be."

I looked out at the square tower that didn't look like a castle worthy of an ancient Irish chieftain. "It's smaller than I remember, like God took a bite out the top of the wall."

"It used to be a fine castle. Never big, but fine. We need to gather money to preserve what's left of it."

"It's in a bad way."

"You'd be in a bad way too if you were built in twelve hundred and seven."

"Fourteen hundred."

"Was it only concentrating on Mary O'Brien you were when you were at school? You certainly weren't concentrating on your history book."

A blast of wind shook the car. The whistle made me shiver, but I still blushed.

"Be careful with Mary," Andrea said.

I turned my face to her. "Why do you say that?"

"She has enough to deal with with her bloody husband, Joe. God help the bastard."

I assumed it was Joe who was 'the bastard'. "I still don't know what you mean."

"Enough." Andrea's voice was calm. "I know why you're here. And it's not for Paul. Or to promote the bloomin' book for that matter."

I gazed out at the waves. Andrea would say her piece whatever I said. I wanted her to talk, to explain to me what I was doing there. Andrea could do that.

"Part of me feels sick when I think of what you're at," she said. "I do, you know. I think, how could you even contemplate such a thing? It's arrogant, it's immoral, it's obscene." She forced her head to rock back. "Plus a load of other shite words you'd probably come up with but I can't even think of now."

Underhand? Exploitative? Deceptive? I didn't share them with Andrea. Instead I picked at the leather on the steering wheel and checked to make sure the keys were still in the ignition, and I waited.

"And another part of me admires your bravery. You must love her very deeply to be acting so horribly callous."

I felt thrashed against the rocks like an Atlantic wave.

"Was it Niamh told you he was dying?"

72

"What's the latest?" I said, keen to change the line of conversation. "Do you know?"

"Palliative care from now on," she said. "Surprised he's lasted so long. Mary is too. Cancer's spread to his bones. In awful pain. His retribution, I think, though Mary would never agree with such a sentiment."

"Why do you say he's a bastard?" I asked.

"Because he is," she whispered. Andrea's head lolled back in the car seat. "It's not my place to explain, but it's never been easy for Mary. And marrying Joe wasn't the smartest thing she ever did, just brought a new set of problems. Problems that got worse over time. Came to a head there middle of last year when she ended up staying the best part of three months at our house. Couldn't live with him. Feared for her life." Andrea's fist clenched in her lap. Her voice remained steady. "She turned up at our back door. Ran away, left him. He'd got drunk and started on at her again. A communion minister he was, holier than thou in public. Just goes to show, no-one knows what goes on behind–"

"He wouldn't hit her?"

She drew in a slow, steady breath. "Capable of it." She coughed to clear her throat. "Can be thick, can Joe ... Anyhow, he got the diagnosis, and she went back to him."

"But why?" I said. "Why go back?"

Andrea sniffed. "Why? It's what women do, they go back. Too many times."

I scoffed. "Neither of my wives came back."

Andrea half laughed. "Were you a bastard too?"

"Good question." I sagged into the car seat, bowed my head. "All I know for sure is I was a drunk."

"Was?" She smiled out the window.

I didn't answer.

"Here is different to England," she said. "Divorce is only legal this last year for a start."

"So I read."

"And it's easier to stay away in England. Too great a shame to it here, yet. Too ugly a stigma to be carrying around with you. Still the fear a woman won't survive without a man, starve to death or something. I had my own share of such prejudicial shite to deal with before I married Sean. But I'm convinced it was Joe's diagnosis that brought Mary back."

Wind buffeted the car. The tangy odour of the sea seeped in through the air vents.

"Templeboy will be better off without him."

"Are they in Templeboy?" I said. "Is that where they live?"

"Back from Kilkenny the last three or four years. Lovely big house. Too big. I told Mary that. Six or seven bedrooms and only the two of them in it? I think they wanted to fill it with the children she couldn't have. She took me round it once, gave me the grand tour. Every bedroom decked out like a child's room, the wallpaper all pinks and blues. Dozens of bloody teddy bears lying around, dolls' houses, toys, gentle crucifixes above the beds like little shrines. And the spookiest thing, the thing that really got me ... That child's bedtime prayer, do you know it? 'Now I lay me down to sleep...' A framed little poster of that in every room. I couldn't believe it. I told her. 'Mary,' I said, 'you're scaring the shite out of me'. I accused her of having the place looking like a playschool where all the children had died and she was waiting for them to return from heaven."

"You didn't say that?"

"Know what she told me? She told me it was all Joe's idea. Just to hammer it home."

"Hammer what home?" I asked.

"Her words were, 'I can no longer conceive and he holds me responsible.' Those were her exact words. He told her it's penance for the sins of the past. And, you know, I think she believed him. It seemed to confirm something for her."

I gave a nervous laugh. "What sins was he on about?"

Andrea started to answer, then stretched for the radio with her left hand. "He's just a bastard." She turned up the volume.

74

25

I have never been a fighter. I had formal training, 'Control and Restraint', found it awkward, lacked coordination, not sure how I passed the assessment. My punch caught Joe in the ear.

He slid alongside the bar a couple of feet but retaliated with a blow to the side of my head that sent me sprawling onto the floor.

Curly Hair yelled from inside the counter.

Joe stood over me. "Ya 'tan bastard," he said and booted me in the belly.

A blurred vision of Curly Hair launched itself from the countertop down onto Joe, tumbling them both over a table.

"Stop it!" Niamh screamed from the doorway. Her heels clattered over the dance floor as she ran towards us.

I worked myself up onto an elbow and touched the sore on my cheek. His sovereign ring had drawn blood.

Curly Hair clambered on top of Joe's chest, pinning him to the floor.

"Let me up," I slurred.

"Move and I'll kick you myself," Niamh said. She bent down and reached towards me.

I swatted her arms away. "Let me up," I shouted, my face and ego bruised.

"Wait," Niamh said, swatting back and winning. "You're bleeding."

Men that probably followed me through school arrived in the bar, talking rapidly, their faces a mix of scowls and smiles, alarmed and amused by the two drunken scrappers.

"Get him off," Joe yelled.

Niamh dabbed my cut with a lace hanky and helped me to my feet.

A tiny crowd of wedding guests milled between me and Joe, their hands splayed towards the floor, pushing the tension into the thin, matted pile of the carpet. Curly Hair maintained his mount until the men reassured him they would look after Joe.

Sean appeared at the door, his lips tight, expression pinched, and strode towards us. I ducked, afraid to meet his eye, and swooned, my head light. The room twisted. The pictures on the walls sliced a curved path towards me. My stomach heaved. I covered my mouth and vomit spewed between my fingers over the counter, and over the floor, and over Niamh.

A young man in a white frilled shirt and glistening-silver cravat stifled a laugh with an arm. Others turned away in disgust at the sight of my whiskey-soaked stomach contents. The air in the bar grew thick with a sickly, sour-sweet odour, like regurgitated baby milk and cigarettes.

Niamh flicked vomit from her face and dangled her hands in the air like an ivory seagull with wounded wings.

Behind the men, Andrea comforted Mary Gullion with an arm around her shoulder.

Mary's glare, delivered between the heads of men in suits, hurt more than any blow Joe could deliver with his boot.

Though it took place before the Vinceman episode, before the drink regained control, before I lost my job and the head-woman had to straighten me out, before Sean's accident, an age ago, a different time, I would never forget about the wedding.

26

"The guy we met first wasn't the best advert for County Hall efficiency, eh, Niamh?" Paul said. "Did the accent throw him? Not the best organised, I thought. His co-worker joins us, and we start to make progress."

"Of sorts," Niamh said.

"At least she had some ideas. It was her came up with the Mother and Baby units."

"Homes," Niamh corrected. "Mother and Baby Homes. It's where the pregnant, unmarried girls were sent. You know Ireland, have the babies elsewhere, avoid the shame on the family, deny it ever happened. Some girls were allowed home, eventually, but not with the baby."

I said, "They think your mother was sent to one of these Homes, to avoid shaming her family?"

"And to pay for her sins," Niamh added. She straightened her back and gave an exaggerated grimace.

"Were they able to tell you your mother's name?" I asked.

Paul gave Niamh a pained glance. "They didn't know anythin' of that detail. Look, they're just formulatin' ideas, brainstormin', thinkin' outside–"

"Your mother's from Sligo," I said. "Is there one of these Homes in Sligo?"

"Everywhere but. They're all over, but none in Sligo. I'm flamin' bewildered by it all to be honest."

Niamh pulled an A4 sheet of lined paper from her coat pocket and smoothed it out on the table. "Your one went away and wrote this. There's nine Homes on this list but she doesn't know if there are others. She thought this might be the best way to find out a name. Then..." Niamh glanced at Paul. "Then there's England. There's a hundred and seventy-two of the places in England."

Paul scrutinised the list of nine. There was a slight, almost imperceptible, shake of his head. He thudded his elbows onto the kitchen table, buried his face in his hands and groaned. He reminded me of a murderer I once supervised who removed a newly-turned jug from the kiln in recreational pottery only to find it collapsed in on itself during firing. Paul spoke through his fingers, "We were advised not to discount England, but my gut says she's here." He rubbed his face. "There's enough to do here in Ireland. It's one of these nine, I know it is. I've less than a fortnight left. Eleven days to chase around all these bloody–"

"Look it's a start, Paul." Niamh picked up the list. "We'll take this to Father Kealey. Paul suggested a local priest, and I think it's a good idea. Father Kealey may know of a priest in Sligo who can help narrow it down."

"Father Brendan Kealey?" I asked.

"Not at all," Niamh said. "He's long gone."

"Father Brendan was as old as God's dad when I lived here."

"His son, Donal," Niamh said smirking.

"Son?"

"He's the same name, so I tease him about being the old priest's son. He hates me for it, but there you go. He's actually no relation at all but it's a lot of fun getting a blush out of him. He's lovely. He'll help if he can. He's handsome too. Not unlike your Father Brendan Kealey, from what I hear. Always thought Donal Kealey in the priesthood a waste of a good man."

Paul grinned. Niamh had lifted him.

"Read out the list," I said.

"Wait, I've glasses." She donned her spectacles. "Not the clearest of writing, but it says…Right, there're homes in Meath, Cork, Westmeath, Tipperary, one, two, three places in Dublin, Tuam in Galway, and Clare."

"You see?" Paul said. "Nothing in Sligo. My birth cert says 'County Sligo'. Say's not a lot else, but it does say 'Sligo'. I'm doubtin' my mother was sent to any of these units."

"But can you trust the certificate, Paul?" I said. "Administration back in the day might have been more a matter of expediency than accuracy."

"You're thinkin' I wasn't born in Sligo?" Paul pushed back from the table.

"We don't know that," Niamh said. "Let's work with what we have."

"So I could've been born anywhere?" His speech slowed. "Even my origin is uncertain? I'm not sure how I feel about not knowin' where I was born." His shoulders slumped. "Didn't know I'd feel like this."

Niamh took slow sips of hot tea. Steam misted her lenses.

Paul recovered. "We need a strategy. First, where to start?"

"Father Donal Kealey," Niamh said, scraping back her chair. "Come on, Flipper, we'll head there now. There's no mass on a Tuesday. He'll just be sitting around reading his theology books. Leave your tea."

"Wait, I'll be with you," I said. They paused and turned to face me. "If you don't mind, that is?"

"No," they both said, one a momentary echo of the other.

I smirked.

Paul turned to Niamh. "Will your mother be 'right on her own? Should she come with us?"

"Not a bother," Niamh said. "No, she enjoys a good rest at this hour and I don't think we'll be long away." She bent over the table, scrunched her nose the way people who wear spectacles sometimes do, and asked me, "Are you sure you're up to meeting him?"

I assumed Niamh was not trying to put me off. She knew of my reservations with new people. "He sounds harmless enough," I said.

79

27

A tall Father Donal Kealey swung open the door. Though he obviously heard us knock he seemed surprised we were there. He looked youthful and fresh, thin eyebrows on a well-shaped, bald and handsome head. A shadow over his lip indicated an ongoing attempt to grow a moustache. His face was friendly, not at all the way I remembered his predecessor, Father Brendan.

Father Donal removed the cigarette that dangled from a side of his mouth, twisted off its hot tip and threw it aside. "I've been off them two and a half years but I've just started again. Trying to kick it into touch before it gets another hold. Well, two years and four months."

Niamh stretched up on her toes and kissed his cheek.

He coloured pink. "Niamh, hello. Why didn't you call before coming over? I've to meet a family at St Patrick's. They've laid a new headstone over the father's grave and they want me to do a blessing."

That reminded me: I needed to call to the cemetery myself.

"Who would that be, then?" Niamh asked, creasing her brow.

"Who? Oh, Andrews. Padraig Andrews, may he rest in peace. From Rathlee."

"Sure he passed over a year ago, didn't he?"

Father Donal said, "Making headstones is a dying trade I'm afraid, Niamh."

I searched his face for a sign of humour. There was none.

"They got it in Leitrim of all places. Drumshanbo must be the gravestone capital of Ireland. Not so far, though, as it should take twelve months to get here. I've ten minutes." He scanned each of our faces before backing inside. "Come on in. Will ye take tea?"

"No, no, no," Niamh said. "Father Donal, this is my uncle over from England."

"Hello." He reached back a hand as we walked through the dark, tiled hallway.

"And this is his friend, Paul McDonnell. From Australia."

"Australia?" Father Donal led us into a small sitting room, one wall sheathed in books with fat spines.

The air was heavy with a musty aroma of macerated vanilla and tobacco. Light from the garden passed through a dissipating cloud of cigarette smoke to fall on the seat of a high-backed damask-covered chair. A copy of *Ulysses*, in a leather sleeve, lay turned over open on the chair's arm. He was two-thirds the way through.

Father Donal waited until we were all inside his reading sanctum before he shook Paul's hand. "Welcome to Ireland."

"Good to be here, Father."

"You're in a hurry," Niamh said. "And we need your help. I'll start talking, ask if you want me to clarify anything."

Niamh spoke. Father Donal, his bald head bowed, listened and nodded at the floor. Paul tried to interject once and failed. I smiled at my niece.

When Niamh had imparted the facts as we knew them, the ticking of an arched wooden clock on the mantelpiece filled the sudden silence. A chill breeze fluttered through an open window, billowing the net curtains like an entering phantom and stirring the hanging smoke. We all looked.

"What if Paul's mother is dead?" I thought.

Father Donal glanced at his watch. "I'll make some enquiries for you, Paul."

"I'd really appreciate that," Paul said. "As Niamh explained, I'm really short on time."

"You need to realise that records will be meagre. I'm not trying to alarm you, but it can be difficult finding out anything

81

in these circumstances. I'm afraid a lot of the adoptions around that time were, shall we say, well-intentioned, but perhaps unregulated. What I mean is, not as thoroughly documented as they ought. You understand what I'm getting at, don't you? Now, I'm sorry Niamh, but I really have to be going."

Father Donal herded us back along the corridor.

Turning back I said, "Father Donal, can I be with you to the graveyard, please?"

He unhooked an overcoat from a rack and sat a wide-brimmed fedora on his head, looking even younger in the hat. He paused, his hands sunk in the pockets of his coat, and scanned the hall table. He dropped a cigarette packet on the table and picked up a small plastic bottle of holy water. "Of course, of course."

28

Why did everyone in Ireland drive too fast?

"I remember the priest before you," I said. "Father *Brendan* Kealey. Often called to the house. He was a great support to my mother."

The car raced towards St Patrick's Cemetery.

"You're from here then, originally?"

"Grew up here," I told him. "I'm Templeboy." My hand gripped the seat.

"Are you *The Harvester* man? Oh, I see now. Congratulations on your literary achievement."

"Thank you," I said. "You've read it?"

"No. So you'd be a brother of Niamh's father?"

I nodded. "The only brother."

"I don't remember you at the funeral."

"No."

I was relieved when Father Donal changed the subject. "He's no relation, no matter what Niamh might have told you. Father Brendan, I mean."

"She thinks a lot of you." Apart from the driving, Father Donal was easy to be with. I felt senior to him, old enough to be his father. I said, "Niamh thought you might be able to help us. I wouldn't have been so hopeful asking old Father Brendan for help." As a conciliatory afterthought, I added, "God rest his soul."

"God rest his soul?" Father Donal turned to face me, eyebrows raised. "The man's not dead at all, yet."

"He must be a hundred years old." I pointed a finger forward at the advancing road.

"Sorry." He swerved the car off the white line. "He's close, late nineties. He's in a nursing home in Sligo. Failed, of course, not the force he used to be, but still mumbles his way through an open mass most Sundays for the residents and staff." Father Donal chortled.

"Retired, surely," I said.

"Catholic priests never retire. A vocation for life. There are people in that home that he has served as priest for over seventy years. Imagine that."

We crunched to a halt next to the cemetery wall.

"Thank God, the family's not here yet." He checked his watch.

"Are people from Templeboy in the home with him, then?" I said. "I bet I'd know some of them."

"No." He checked the rearview mirror. "I meant the people who were in his parish in Sligo. He covered a large slice of Sligo town did Father Brendan, as well as Templeboy. Thankfully, the Bishop readjusted the boundaries about twelve years ago, so I rarely have to venture into Sligo now. No, people didn't realise how hard Father Brendan worked, in his day. A flock of over two thousand, him on his own, overseeing everything from burials and marriages to—"

"Blessing bicycles and child adoptions," I said.

Father Donal glared at me.

"There's a chance," I said. "If Paul McDonnell's mother was in his parish in Sligo, Father Brendan would've known of her."

"He wouldn't remember that far back. Nineteen-fifty-eight, Niamh said. I really don't think—"

"But it's worth a try."

"Look, it's a lot to expect a man of that age to recall anything. Him in the early stages of dementia and all. I'd be reluctant to bother him with this, in all honesty. He's not in the best of health."

"Doesn't a dementia sufferer often remember the distant past better than what happened yesterday?"

"He barely remembers the words to the Lord's Prayer, I'm afraid. Here's the family now." He sounded relieved. "To work. Will you be wanting a lift back?"

I knew it wasn't an offer. "No. No, I think I'd like to walk. Reacquaint myself with the place."

Father Donal had retrieved his hat from the back seat and got out of the car before I finished speaking. Stones scraped on the tarmac as he strode off.

The family were in the wing mirror, each wrapped in a thick coat. The men wore ties; the women wore hats. They dipped at the waist as they shook hands with the young priest.

I went in search of my brother's grave.

29

"So he can't help?" Paul said.

"Or won't," I said. "Reckons old Father Brendan's too old and too ill to remember anything."

"Then let's pick one of these units and we'll start visitin'. Ask some questions, see what we can find out."

"Homes, Paul," Niamh said. "They're Mother and Baby *Homes*, not units. And be aware that some of them may no longer exist."

Paul sighed. "We need to make a start. I'm concerned I'm runnin' out of time here and still not within a bull's roar of getting' any answers. It's like I'm swimmin' up against rocks at every stroke."

"I think we should meet with old Father Brendan Kealey," I said. "But we can't do it immediately, we'd need Father Donal's agreement. Niamh?"

"I'll have a word with him. He's busy with mid-week masses tomorrow, but Thursday, I'll be on to him."

"In the meantime, we'll start on the Homes?" Paul said. "Do we know if *any* are still goin'?"

"We can check the list," Niamh said.

"Thanks for helpin'. I appreciate it." Paul laid a hand on Niamh's wrist. "You and I could call a few of them, phone around?"

"Pick the one nearest Sligo," I said. "You and I maybe visit it, Paul?"

"Sure. You got a map book or somethin', Andrea, please?"

Andrea gave an absent smile and nodded but remained silent.

Niamh stood up. "I'll get it."

30

Next morning I left Niamh guiding Paul around Ireland, plotting the locations of Mother and Baby Homes on a worn and creased map with a tear along its centre fold.

I parked by the front gate and sat in the car biting nails and wringing hands, deliberating the wisdom of my actions. Was this what I wanted? Was it what she'd want? I loosened my coat zip, took two long breaths and thumped the car horn with a fist. I cringed at the cliché.

We drove to Enniscrone. I bought us each a wafer of ice-cream and we sat on a damp wooden bench at the edge of the beach.

I licked my fingers clean and sat erect, my chest out, and looked for activity on the sand to give my attention to. It was deserted. "I'm sorry to hear about Joe," I said. My voice sounded deeper than usual.

"I love when the sea dances like that," Mary said. "In, two three. Out, two three. An old-time waltz."

The water formed foamy surf where it made land, a perfect white arc in Killala Bay. Over the bay, the mountain of Nephin, forever dark and magisterial, still dominated the distant horizon.

"He's not long left. They're just treating the pain. I don't want him to die in pain." She popped the last of her ice-cream into her mouth and wiped her fingers with a tissue. "It has been quite a while since I last ate one of them."

I gave a slow nod. "I'm here if you need me, Mary. Anything at all." That was what I wanted her to know, that I was here for her.

She turned her head, the muscles in her cheek tight. "You weren't here forty years ago when I needed you."

87

I stopped my mouth from gaping. People seemed to enjoy pointing out my failures to attend. Confrontation was not what I wanted.

"Why didn't you think to make contact?" Mary said. "When I came back you'd just disappeared. No message, nothing. Not even a letter."

My leg fidgeted, my heel drumming the sand. It was her that left me. I didn't want to argue with Mary. Not with Mary. "Wasn't it *you* that went away?" I said. "Off to join the Holy Sisters of Calcutta or someplace. A nun, remember? Your mother said you went off to join an order. Dublin, she said. First I heard about you wanting to become a nun." A lump thickened in my throat, too late to stop the angry words escaping.

Her eyes roved my face. She didn't look angry, more full of pity. She picked at the cuticle of a thumb. "It would have cost you nothing to get in touch." She cast a wry smile to the sand. "Did you forget we were to get married?" She stopped picking and slid her fingers beneath her thighs. She rocked forward on the bench, shoulders hunched, and raised her head to look out to sea.

I scoffed, then regretted it. "Your mother said you were gone for good, never to be seen again. Made out it was all my fault. I had images of you feeding the black babies out in Somalia. Didn't think you'd ever be back."

"Black babies in Somalia? With the Sisters of Calcutta? Aren't those two locations–"

"I know."

"–a few thousand miles apart?" Her smile eased the tension. "Did you hate me?" she asked. A breeze shifted a curled strand of hair in front of her face.

A breath I didn't realise I was holding escaped. "I wouldn't know how to hate you ... Your mother hated *me*, though, that was obvious."

Mary straightened her spine and threw back her head. "Yes, my mother. God love her." She chuckled. "I told you once, do you remember, when she found out about you, that she was fond of you?"

"I remember," I said.

"I lied. She wasn't fond of you at all. She bore an intense dislike of your father for reasons I couldn't figure out at that time."

"He was a useless drunk?"

"You were a 'bad sort' according to her." Mary affected an old-Sligo accent, the vowels clipped and rapid. "Lie down with dogs and you'll get up with fleas." It was the piercing voice of her mother, back from the dead. Mary's cheeks dimpled. "She knew well I was engaging in a bit of illicit courting. When someone from the village told her it was with *you*, my God." She squinted against the breeze. "She didn't want me cycling with you. Threatened to set fire to my new bike." Mary rocked forward on her seat, laughing. "I told her she couldn't because old Father Kealey had blessed it, and it would be a mortal sin."

We both laughed.

"And if she did, she'd burn in hell along with it."

I watched Mary talk the way I used to watch her, enjoying the melody of her voice. Nothing around us mattered. I wanted her to talk forever. For time to stop and forever to start now. I yearned to touch her.

"You'll never guess what she told me, though."

"Go on," I said.

"You ready for this?"

I nudged her arm, more a lingered press. "Go on."

"My mother and your father stepped out together."

I coughed out a laugh. "Yes, I can well imagine that." ·

White teeth were visible between her smiling red lips. "According to my mother, they were very much in love."

"Mary, you're clearly intoxicated on the smell of the seaweed. I remember a time when you could handle the sea air."

"You don't believe me, do you?"

"Why would I?" I felt a little giddy. "After what your mother said to me?"

"She told me before she died. One of our last mother-and-daughter conversations."

"You cannot be serious?"

"Solemn oath. How did she put it?" Old-Sligo returned. "He was the handsomest laddeen in the county."

"My father? And your mother? I can't see it."

"Doesn't end there." Mary rolled her head towards me. Her smile turned sad. "Mammy told me that your father went and got another girl pregnant."

"Who, for God's sake?"

"Your mother."

"What?" I tried to blink away the lightheadedness.

"That'd be you, then," she mocked. "You're the reason your parents married."

"Jesus, are you honestly telling me the truth?"

"She thought it a mistake."

I stared into the sand. "My mother and father?" My chest tightened.

"Mammy thought getting married like that was the wrong thing to do."

"These are my parents you're talking about."

"Never thought I'd be having that conversation with my mother, I must admit. And I'm only telling you what she told me." Mary pulled her coat tight around her. "It might not be true, but I'd say it is ... Were they happy, your mother and father?"

"Bloody hell, I don't know. I suppose." I shrugged. "Yes. Yes, they seemed ... Happy enough." I recalled the middle-of-the-night conversation, my father urinating his poitín onto the rain-soaked grass. Lonely in love? Is that what he was telling me that night, he married the wrong woman? "My father and your mother?" I laughed at the irony. Mary laughed with me.

The waltzing Atlantic waves pushed ashore memories of cycling to Enniscrone Beach with Mary. The sand, the wind, the sea, had shifted in a million tides but were the same. Nephin had not stirred. My feelings for Mary were still there, had never left. My heart ached. I reached an arm across the gap between us and rested it on her shoulder, unsure of what I was doing.

She didn't flinch but drooped her head. Curls curtained her cheek. "My mother told me she watched you destroy your ring."

"Oh, the hazel ring. I remember." My arm felt misplaced, but I didn't want to break contact. "Only an old wooden thing."

In the middle distance a black Labrador with a green collar flicked up wet sand racing full pelt at a resting seagull. The bird flapped and lifted into the air. The dog wheeled and trotted back, its tail held high, philosophical about the lost opportunity.

"Is that what you thought? When I heard about the ring, I knew you hated me and would never come back from England."

"Mary, I didn't hate you. I was mad. Angry as hell. I blamed your mother for your leaving. I wanted to destroy something, hurt her back the way she hurt me. We were children."

"We were," she said. "We were just children."

I squeezed her shoulder.

She said, "That's why it meant so much."

"I wanted to ask at the wedding," I said. "About the nun stuff. Where did all that come from? You never told *me* anything about you wanting to become a nun. You didn't act as if you did."

She turned her head. The fall of hair was fine enough for me to examine a side and the front of her face. Faint creases at the outer corner of her eye, from when she used to smile, feathered out towards her cheek and up towards her temple. Deeper lines, what my mother called "a woman's worry lines", gathered above her nose and ran into the creases on her brow. Lipsticked lips underlined the neat nose, their peaks and curves intimately familiar. She carried the marks of age well, her balanced poise retained.

Mary peered out over the water. She inhaled deeply, her breasts straining her coat. She tucked hair behind an ear and dislodged my arm with a subtle shrug of a shoulder. "Yes, the wedding," she said. "Bloody, hell."

I hid my humbled hand in a pocket.

"What possessed the two of you to go fighting?" she said.

The heat of a blush in my cheeks battled the chill of the beach wind. "You know, I don't even remem–"

"A couple of drunken eejits, the pair of you. Embarrassed everyone. Especially your poor brother, Sean, God rest him. Your niece's wedding for Christ's sake."

I thought she was about to mention my absence from Sean's funeral. I didn't want her to get angry. "Not my proudest–"

"You know Joe blamed me for that, don't you?" Mary said.

"Our squabble? Why blame you?"

"He made sure I paid for it too."

I was losing her. I wanted to place my arm back on her shoulder, to wrap it around her, to pull her tight to me. I wanted the talking to stop, time was passing. I wanted to kiss her.

"That was the first time he struck me," she said.

"Mary–"

"That night, after the fight with you."

"Mary, I'm sorry. If I did anything to cause that, I'm sor–"

"My mother encouraged him, you know?"

I slumped back on the bench seat.

"'She's flighty,' she'd tell him." The deep-Sligo accent again but without humour. "A firm hand'll keep her in check. Stop her strayin' on ya." Mary crossed her legs. Her skirt rode up her thigh exposing a knee. "She told him all about us. Everything."

"We were children, Mary. What could she tell, anyhow?"

Mary gazed at where the dog padded away through puddled sand, but her eyes were dull and fixed on a point that vanished out in the ocean. Her red lips curled into a sad smile. She whispered, as if to herself, so quiet I could barely hear. She might have said, "You don't know the half of it."

31

"I think Mammy's trying to put me off Paul."

"Pardon?"

Niamh and I sat in the car, waiting.

"Thinks I might run away with him." She laughed. "To bloody Australia."

"You serious?"

"No. But she does seem a bit conflicted about him. On the one hand she seems to enjoy his company then, last night, she told me she thought he was 'too presumptuous'."

"Presumptuous? Might have a point."

"Says he's a bit too forward for her liking. Warned me to stay clear."

"And what do *you* think about *staying clear*?"

She slapped my shoulder. "Shut up and stop teasing."

Paul and Niamh? There would be implications for Andrea. "Your mother needs you here."

Niamh's smile slipped. She cocked her head.

"How would she cope?" I said.

Niamh tutted. "We'll end this conversation now, shall we?" She almost folded her arms across her chest but checked herself. She bridged the silence before it grew to a chasm. "At first I thought this was all a bit of a game, this search for Paul's mother. A secret little scandal, a bit of intrigue. But since you arrived, since I've met Paul … This means a lot. This'll affect people's lives."

"It could affect people's lives more than we'd like," I said, relieved she was still bothered to talk to me. "There's the mother to consider, if we find her, her family, but especially this man."

Paul skipped down the ramp from the front door. "Sorry to keep you guys."

Niamh manoeuvred herself out of the car seat. "Here, sit in."

"Shame you're not comin'," Paul said.

"I'll stay with Mammy. She needs me here, apparently. No, I'll do some phoning around and speak to Father Donal. Mary Gullion's coming over later. She and Mammy'll have one of their Ladies' Afternoons."

"Do I know Mary Gullion?" Paul said.

"I doubt it," Niamh said. "But Mr Righteous behind the steering wheel can tell you a thing or two about her."

The trip to the beach with Mary hadn't ended well. Mary's mood altered after talking about her mother, laughing one minute, quiet the next. I didn't know what to say, or how to recover it. We returned to the car, citing the chill breeze as the reason. Mary refused my pitiful offer of tea and cake in a stone-fronted café at the end of Cliff Road. By the time I dropped her home she was anxious to get to the hospital to visit Joe, car keys already in her hand. There was no embrace when we parted, no kiss goodbye, no promise to meet again. Nothing. And even if such gestures were the least I had hoped for I could no longer think of a reason why I should have hoped for anything at all.

I still found it hard to believe what she told me about my father and her mother. Her mother had a lot to answer for.

I cranked the engine. "We need to get on."

"Did I interrupt somethin'?" Paul said.

"Not at all," Niamh said.

Paul folded his frame into the front seat, closed the door and lowered the window. "We'll see you tomorrow."

"Miss you 'till then," Niamh said. She bent down to the window, I thought, to kiss Paul. Her cleavage was on show.

I looked away.

"Do you like Chinese food?" she said. "There's a new Chinese restaurant in Sligo. It's gone very cosmopolitan here all of a sudden."

"Love Chinese," Paul said. "My treat, though."

"When you're back, then…Safe journey."

I steered the car onto the road and pointed it towards Ballina. Niamh came to the gate and waved as we drove away.

We made good time on the quiet roads, passing through Ballina, crossing Lough Conn and through the flat and wild boglands of Cunnagher More, hidden that morning in a dense and intimidating mid-summer mist. We entered Castlebar on the Pontoon Road, just over an hour after leaving Templeboy. I wanted to call into another library, to find information about The Lawn, the residence of Lord Lucan in the nineteenth century.

"The next book?" Paul asked.

The librarian made photocopies of maps dated 1838 and folded them into an envelope. She suggested I buy a copy of John Murray's *Handbook for Travellers in Ireland*, from 1878. I wrote the title in my notepad though I didn't hold out much hope of sourcing Murray's book. I bought sandwiches instead.

"You need one of these, mate," Paul said handing me a napkin. He pointed to his lip.

I wiped salad cream from the corner of my mouth.

Two hours later we approached Galway city. Johnny Madden drew another eclectic mix of items to a close on his radio show without any mention of my interview. The programme's rolling discussion was the validity of a recent report comparing the Irish economy with that of the 'raging tiger' economies of East Asia.

Paul told the radio, "I've ridden the Asian tiger, and Ireland don't want one."

The item concluded with a consensus that thanks to the robust financial propriety of the Irish banking system, Ireland was ready for its own 'Celtic Tiger'.

Paul huffed and shook his head.

It went straight to the news. I remembered who the voice reminded me of. The newsreader sounded like a younger Mary. She told us that at the ongoing trial of Patrick Gillaney, now being held at Dublin Circuit Criminal Court, Gillaney's mother-in-law died from a heart attack as she was about to give her evidence on the stand. The case was becoming a spectacle.

I turned off the radio. "Your father," I said. "Have I asked you about your father? Any mention of your father on the birth certificate?"

Paul took a while to answer. "You did ask, long ago. No name. A diagonal line across the box. Just Sligo. That's all it says, along with my first name and my date of birth. Reminds me of a Friday-afternoon document where the clerk pissed off early for the weekend, came back Monday and started on the next certificate. It just says 'Sligo'."

"Nineteen-fifty-eight?"

"Nineteen-fifty-eight. Though I'm startin' to doubt even that."

The year after my family left Ireland. "Why are we heading to Cork?" I asked.

Paul slouched in his seat, his knees pushed up against the dashboard. "Look," he said. He sat up straight again, unable to settle, and reached into the footwell for his canvas bag. "I've got the list of units here. You said find one that's still going. This is all we could find."

"The nearest to Sligo?"

"The only bloody one." He opened his bag and removed the list of homes. "See. St Patrick's, closed nineteen-fifty-eight. Sean Ross Abbey, closed nineteen-seventy. Manor House, closed nineteen-seventy-one. St Rita's Nursing Home in Dublin, closed in the seventies. They're all bloody closed."

"Alright," I said. "Take it easy."

"I'm running out of time." He spread the fingers of a hand wide in frustration. "The book. You mention Sligo in *The*

Harvester. I knew you lived there from the way you described it. Thought you'd be able to help. Thought you'd know the people. I thought you might even know my mum." He stuffed the list back into the bag. "Figured you're both about the same age. But it all sounds bloody ridiculous now I say it out loud."

My chest tightened in embarrassment.

Paul carefully retrieved another folded sheet. "I'm thirty-nine years old and I've never met my mum. I thought you'd solve it for me." He unfolded the paper on his lap. "You were a detective after all."

"I was not a detective. Why do people think–? Is that your birth certificate?"

"For what it's worth," he said.

The road ahead was blocked, I slowed the car. A stocky man in a donkey jacket with 'Electricity Supply Board - ESB' printed across his shoulders walked in the middle of the road. Before him a flock of sheep filled the carriageway.

"Listen," Paul said. "I'm sorry. I apologise."

"Don't."

"Yes, I need to. You come to Ireland to help me find my mum and I'm actin' mad as a cut snake."

I smiled at his simile.

"I'm soundin' like an ungrateful bastard."

More accurate. "It's fine."

"I'm not used to failure."

"You've not failed yet."

"No. No, you're right. Not yet. And I do feel closer to her here in Ireland. Closer than I've ever felt." He scrubbed at the back of his neck. "That must make no sense to you."

Donkey Jacket kept walking. No hurry. His dog glanced back as our car neared.

I nodded. To Paul, not the dog. I anticipated what was coming and reached to turn the radio back on.

"Mother died when I was thirty. My adoptive mother. Didn't really bother me before, but I've thought about my birth mum more since that happened. A friend reckons her death gave me permission, like I wouldn't hurt her by seekin' out my mum. I don't think my mother would've minded. I've always known, my parents told me I was adopted from the beginnin'. They were always straight with me."

His sentences had taken on a rising tonal inflection that made them sound like questions. Cars grew in my rear-view mirror. I was trapped in a pseudo interrogation.

"Debbie and I separated a month later."

His wife. Ex-wife.

"Not because of it. We'd just … Anyway, it was a rough-arsed time."

I understood marital separations and the accompanying 'rough-arsed' times. That was a question I had a reply for.

"I've two younger brothers," Paul continued. "They're biological siblings and good people, it's just … Since mother died, and Debbie, and me hittin' my thirty-crisis, all that shit, that's when I started looking around me and I noticed it. Know what I noticed?"

I shook my head.

"They all look alike. The family. My brothers look like my father and act like my mother. I don't. Hair's the wrong colour for a start. I'm the odd one. The cuckoo in the nest. Do you say that? I read it on the plane over, thought it fit."

"I think I know what you mean."

Donkey Jacket gave a sharp whistle and raised an arm. The dog darted left flank and disappeared over a ditch.

Paul said, "My father's dead."

I looked at him, confused. "What? Which father?"

"Birth father. I know he's dead."

"You know that, how?"

"A few years ago, I got a feelin'."

"A feeling?"

"In my gut."

"So you don't know?"

"That's how it is with me. Don't ask how, it just is. Like a hunger pain. Not even a hunger pain, more the feelin' you get in the middle of a long run when you've burnt up your glycogen and your fuel pump switches to consuming fat. For a couple of minutes you just want to stop and puke."

He was blathering. I made no sense of it.

The sheep twisted back and forth, their way barred, also confused.

"I'm sure you think it's nonsense, but I'm just as instinctive in business. It's the way I am. Got a similar feelin' when my marriage died, a whole year before we split. I just knew how things were goin' to play out."

Dying marriages, more familiar territory. I wanted to ask about his business more than about his dead father or his dead marriage. I halted the car.

Donkey Jacket inched forward in half-steps, crouching, arms spread, coaxing his flock.

"Leaves me feelin' I've no roots," Paul said. "No identity." He played his fingertips over the birth certificate. "That's the big one for me, identity. I've none. Friends ask about attachment to my adoptive family, and there is, sure there is, but they're McDonnells by birth. That's the difference, I'm only one on paper. This scrap of a document is my only source of identity. And the box that says 'Sligo' now looks to be bullshit." He gazed at the sheep. "Does any of this make any sense?"

It didn't, but I nodded.

"I don't belong. It's not their fault, it's just … I'd like to know where I do belong. If my birth father's dead, I need to find my birth mum. I need to find some identity. Before it's too late."

The sheep streamed into a gateway at the side of the road, their heads up, black feet trotting. The dog reappeared on the road ahead of them. Donkey Jacket leaned and touched its ears. The dog wagged its tail and raised its snout at us, as if apologising for the delay.

"She's still alive, I know she is. I want to talk to her. See what she is." Paul folded away the certificate. "Just meet her is all. Tell her I understand why she did what she did."

The pseudo questions made him sound more vulnerable. I wanted to tell him that things would work out, but an unexpected lump in my throat choked the words off.

The car accelerated through automatic gears, pushing us back into our seats.

He dropped the bag between his feet. "But like you, I think I've Buckley's of finding her in Cork." He wiped his eyes with a palm.

I opened my mouth to ask who Buckley was, a question of my own, but Paul turned the radio on loud.

We skirted Galway and pushed on towards Limerick. In Limerick we ate in a busy pub. I was determined not to drink but washed down a satisfying fish meal with a glass of whiskey. Paul flexed a disapproving eyebrow. I ignored him.

"So what's Niamh's story?" he said shoving away his plate.

"Her story?"

"Can't believe she's not married."

"It would be difficult, her mother the way she is."

Paul huffed. "Surely it's more contingent on Niamh meetin' the right guy rather than on her mother's condition?"

He lacked the Irish sense of responsibility.

"No. No, her sister married first and left the family home. A couple of years later her step-father, my brother, died and Andrea took ill. Niamh's been her mother's carer ever since."

Paul smiled and shook his head. "I see … She's a good sort, I know that much."

"She's the best sort," I said. "Her mother depends on her for everything. Why do you ask, anyway?"

"Just wonderin', that's all." He picked a burnt-brown chip from his plate.

32

We reached Cork six hours after leaving Templeboy and halted outside what looked like a reasonable bed and breakfast on Lower Glanmire Road, next to the River Lee. I asked Paul to book us in and enquire about parking. A twisting network of concrete ramps and flyovers, leading trucks to Tivoli Docks, blocked any view of the river from the car.

Paul stopped and spoke to the first pedestrian he met on the footpath. The woman nodded and raised an arm to point.

"Drive on," Paul said, fixing his seat belt. "My treat."

"Where we going?"

At the end of an avenue of semi-detached houses we passed between two stout brick piers and onto a block-paved driveway. Gardeners tended lawns and trimmed trees. A small team of workmen shovelled sand from a barrow by the boundary wall. A tall, scantily-leaved ash tree curved like a seductive belly dancer in the middle of a neat, grassy island.

"Opened last year," Paul said. "Not quite finished by the look of it, but the reviews are excellent. Hope they can fit us in."

Two brass plaques guarded the hotel's entrance, a crescent of five stars on each.

I deposited my bag on a bed with a mahogany headboard as tall as the mattress was long and met Paul in the bar. A turf fire burned needlessly in a tile-and-granite Victorian fireplace.

"You mind if I have a scout around?" Paul asked.

"That's fine," I said and signalled the barman, a young Pakistani student with a Cork accent, to serve me another drink.

We'd made no arrangement to meet for dinner, and I doubted I had the clothes to dress appropriately, so I left the hotel. I needed a sleep, but first I needed a proper drink. I called into a pub with a horseshoe-shaped bar, around the corner on Bandon Road.

I drank alone and brought a half-bottle back to my room, smuggling it into the hotel as though it was prisoner contraband.

I awoke sweating, fully clothed. The same nightmare. Vinceman dragged me into his cell and shoved me against the wall. His arm dripped blood. He grinned then turned his head to another doorway, a concealed doorway, one I'd never seen on any plan of the prison or during any cell inspection. Joe Gullion stood in the opening holding a shard of metal, one end wrapped with a cloth as a handle. Joe said something to Vinceman about me being no good to Mary now. I'd had the same dream dozens of times in the previous two years, but the secret doorway was always a shock and I still couldn't make out Joe's exact words.

I eased the ache in my head by adding the remnants of the whiskey to my tea and sat on the edge of the unused bed until the nausea passed, massaging my kidneys.

In the breakfast room I watched Paul consume enough food for both of us. I finished my black coffee and we got up to leave for Blackrock.

A bell-boy in a pillbox hat, trimmed to match his navy silver-buttoned jacket, followed Paul to the car holding aloft plastic bags draped from hangers.

"Met the proprietors last night," Paul said. "Lovely couple. Arranged for my clothes to be laundered. Couldn't find you."

The bell-boy nodded me a wink after pocketing his tip.

Blackrock, formerly an isolated fishing village but now a suburb of Cork city, lay due east of the hotel.

"There, other side of that roundabout." Paul leaned forward, one hand on the dashboard. "Stop the car. Please."

I pulled to the side of the road in the midst of an industrial business park. A well-manicured tree-lawn fell away behind a low wall to a brown-brick office block to our right. Beyond it a tall chimney billowed thick clouds of steam into the air. A line of tall trees, maple and beech, crowded the other side of the road. There was a background drone of busy factory machines. Spits of rain spotted the windscreen.

Paul pointed ahead. "That's it there, the blue sign."

Another sign, to the left, showed a silhouette of two children, blue images on a green rolling background. One child draped a leg out of the green as though perched on the bough of a tree.

"Looks friendly enough." My voice had a brave sobriety, but sweat pushed out of my forehead and the steering wheel felt clammy in my grip. I pressed a button on the door handle and the window descended a fraction. A whiff of freshly-baked biscuits wafted in through the gap.

"Okay," Paul said. "I'm ready, let's go."

"You sure?"

He nodded.

I steered the car through the narrow opening and drove towards the barrier. Damp gravel crunched beneath the tyres.

The security guard folded away his newspaper, picked up a clipboard and stepped out of a square, grey portacabin. He wore a peaked cap, a glowing yellow coat, and teal trousers. He held up a palm as we approached.

I lowered my window fully.

"How a' ye, lads?" the guard said, bending. He smelled of tobacco. "Welcome to the Blessborough Centre." The voice was soft, mellifluous, his words elongated.

Birds in the overhanging trees bickered and chirped their frustrations at the weather.

Paul leaned across and said, "Paul McDonnell. Here to see Dr Fitzgerald."

The guard creased his brow. "Dr Fitzgerald, ya say?"

"Yea, I've a meetin'?"

"Right." The security guard straightened to consult the clipboard and mumbled as he slid a finger down his sheet of paper. His face appeared beside me again. "You're not on the lisht, Mr McDonnell."

"Strewth, we've driven miles. Look, I spoke to Dr Fitzgerald's secretary."

"Do you have an oul' name for the secretary?"

"No," Paul answered. "But I only spoke to her a couple of days ago."

"I dare say ya did, son, I dare say ya did." The guard peered out from under the raindrop-dappled peak. "But ya see, the trouble is, you're not on the lisht."

"Call his office," Paul said. "Speak to the secretary, she'll tell you."

"They don't like me to be botherin' them much up at the main house, now."

"You can call can't you?" Paul pleaded. "We've driven all the way from County Sligo."

"They do be busy enough up at the house to be honesht. An' that's without havin' to be answerin' phone calls from the likes of me. I'm afraid there's no entry unless you're on the lisht, now. An' if ya had an appointment, your name'd surely be there."

Paul slapped the dash, spilling his papers into the footwell.

"Did you make an appointment?" I asked. The damp air cooled my face.

"Spoke to the secretary on the phone," Paul said. "Or Niamh did. One of us. She knew we were comin'."

"But did you make an appointment?" I insisted.

Paul shook his head and sat back in his seat. "Maybe not."

"That would explain it, now," the guard said.

I said, "We'll make an appointment and call back."

The guard smiled under his peak. "Grand. I'll be on the lookout for yer name on the lisht, so."

"I reckon she only agreed because we'd driven so far," Paul said.

We were in Callanan's Bar, on the corner of George's Quay and Mary Street. I didn't know a George; I did know a Mary. On our second pint. 'Hair of the dog that shit on you', my father called it.

"Had to summon all my powers of persuasion to talk her into lettin' us in at all."

We were committed to spending another night in Cork. Paul used his mobile phone to book us back into the hotel and to call Niamh. I said a few words to her myself. The device was heavier than I expected. "Handy enough, them things," I said.

"Everyone'll carry one soon," Paul said.

"Can't see that. Not everyone thinks they're so important they need to be contactable every second of the day. You have the secretary's name, haven't you?"

"Finola Dawkins. But she won't be there. We're meetin' Dr Fitzpatrick and Sister Agnes Brown. Apparently, we're fortunate Dr Fitzpatrick's there on a Saturday. We have twenty minutes and no more. All very formal."

"I thought you said his name was Dr Fitzgerald."

"I got it wrong." He sipped his pint. "And Dr Fitzpatrick is a woman. She's Director of the Blessborough Centre."

"No bloody wonder the security guard wouldn't let us in," I said. "The place full of vulnerable adults and children and you at the gate asking for names you just plucked out of your arse."

Paul laughed. "Bloody ridiculous, I accept. Look, I apologise for my incompetence. I'd make a hopeless appointments secretary."

"What *do* you do for a living?" I asked.

"You won't believe me."

"All you've told me is that you're a businessman. What business has to put up with the likes of you?"

"I own hotels in Sydney."

"Own?"

"And Melbourne."

My jaw dropped. "You serious?"

"And in Taiwan," he said.

"Taiwan? How many altogether?"

"We have eight. Currently. The one in Taipei is quite smart, you get good views of Taipei 101 from the roof-top restaurant. Mind, you can see that bloody skyscraper from everywhere in the city."

"Who's we?" I asked, leaning forward on my stool.

"Me and two partners. My younger brother runs the finances. He's the spreadsheet jockey. Then there's Brett, who's a bloody liability, but we love him too much to cut him loose."

"Hotels…" It explained his interest in the five star. "What took you into Taiwan?"

"One of the Asian Tiger economies, mate. The Little Dragons." He made claws with his hands. "Rapid infrastructure development, vibrant export market, well-educated workforce, low taxes. Economic conditions couldn't get any better. So instead, they got worse."

"The crash. I read about it."

"Taiwan was the most robust of them, we thought. Turns out we were right. When it all went nipples-skyward it scared the shit out of us, but we come through pretty much unscathed. Actually in the process of buyin' another one there at the moment. It's why I need to get back, some bullshit papers need signing." He checked his enthusiasm. "Enough of me." He lifted his glass to hide a modest blush. "Tell me about life as a prison guard. Met some rough'uns I bet? You did well to cope in that environment, don't think I would."

My life as a prison guard. Did I cope? I didn't know where to start. The few good memories? The many bad? Working in a bolted, confined atmosphere of hate and mistrust? And that's just amongst my colleagues. Ha!

Paul's face mirrored my smile. "I see you enjoyed it. Rewardin' right? Bet you got some stories out of it too?"

I considered telling him about Vinceman and the near-death encounter that ended my quarter-century career. That's a story, right, mate?

Paul's smile faded.

The incident that defined me. Made me who I am. Nearly destroyed me. The beermat muffled the rattle of the empty glass as I placed it down. I took a slow deep breath, anxious for Paul not to notice, smelled smoke and beer and body odour. I pulled at my fingers and tuned in to traffic noises from the street. "Nothing to tell," I said to a beer stain on my shoe.

Paul swallowed the rest of his pint and left the table. When he returned with two more drinks, he lightened the mood. "Great runnin' route. Along these quays, next to the river. Flat."

"Not in the rain it ain't," I said. "Great pub-crawl route."

We laughed.

The tremor passed, the Beamish warmed and relaxed me. It felt comfortable sitting, drinking, laughing with Paul. I found him generous and easy company, personable and amiable. Traits conducive, no doubt, to a successful career in hotels and hospitality. I wasn't sure how successful he was going to be in the search for his birth mother. We still had time. Enough time?

"Some nice pubs along this stretch," I said. "This is a great little place."

"You're fond of the pubs I've noticed. I'd be a ton weight if I downed the grog like you."

"Hear now the pot blackguarding the kettle," I pronounced.

Paul smiled. "You write that?"

John Steinbeck wrote it. And he probably stole it from someone else. I didn't tell Paul any of that but picked up my fresh pint and nodded a cheers. "I suppose it's the running that keeps your weight off?"

"Yea, cheers, mate. That and the swimmin'. And the cyclin' of course. Weight and stress, exercise keeps them at bay. Need to ramp it up when I get back, Ireland puts pounds on you."

107

"I used to be a lanky streak like you once, believe it or not." I became conscious of the fold of belly falling over my waistband. "What do you weigh?" I asked and immediately regretted it; I wasn't going to come out of this exchange well.

"Eighty-three kilos before comin' over."

I must have looked confused.

"In your money a little over thirteen stone," he said. "You?"

"More than that."

"We're equal in height, but I can't imagine you thin. What's the lightest you ever been?" He lifted his glass to his mouth.

"Seven pounds three ounces."

He snorted beer up his nose and jerked back on his seat, coughing and spluttering and slopping his drink.

"In your money about three kilograms." I hooked a knee up into clasped hands and reclined on my stool, pleased with his reaction to the old joke. "You alright?"

"Nearly bloody drowned on me piss," he said laughing. He wiped his mouth with the back of a thumb.

I laughed back. I wanted this man to find his birth mother. In that moment I knew that we would find her. I needed to tell Paul an Irish barman would not appreciate his calling beer 'piss', 'grog' was bad enough. Instead I said, "I want to apologise for what I said. The day we met. At the airport. The Aboriginal Australians. I meant no disrespect. I'm not always like that."

Paul scrutinized me, then said, "A misunderstood people. Don't make it right, what you said, but I'm afraid you're no different to most."

"I'm sorry."

Paul sucked air through his teeth. "Sure." He bounced a knee. "And also, I like to think *this is* my country."

"It is," I said and sipped my beer. To recover the mood I said, "We're going to find your mum, Paul." I believed it.

He settled, and he coughed into a fist. "Yea ... Thanks. With your help, I think we will. And Niamh's help. And Andrea of course." He leaned forward over the table and nudged a damp beermat back and forth with a finger. "I'm not doin' all this to upset anyone."

"I know."

"I'd just like to …"

"I know." I needed to prepare him. "But what if she doesn't want to see you?"

"I've thought about that."

"You have?"

"Christ, yes. She may have family who don't know about me. An old fella she hasn't told. I'm not here to break that up." He pinned the beermat down with his finger. "I believe she will be in some pain. I want to tell her it's okay, what she did. Put an arm around her and tell her it's alright. She's my mum. I'm not here for anythin', but I'll take whatever she gives me." He sniffed, wiped his face and stood up. "My new bloody trousers are destroyed with beer stains, ya bastard. Look at the state of them." He ran his hands down his thighs. "Listen … Ya bastard … You got me all …" He blinked and blew air through pursed lips. "Why do you think they're reluctant to meet us?"

"You mean at Blessborough? It would be a help if we got their names right when we called to the gate."

"Quite right, my fault. I accept full responsibility." His chest swelled as he inhaled deeply. "I owe the gateman an explanation."

"Think back to what Father Donal Kealey said. If adoptions went on in places like Blessborough, they probably *were* well-intentioned. Completely unregulated, but well-intentioned. Now they've just become an embarrassment."

Paul shrugged. "You think we'll find anything out about Mum tomorrow?"

"Now that we have an appointment, at least we'll be on the *lisht.*"

33

"I owe you a bloody apology, mate," Paul said.

"For what?"

"A big bloody apology. For wastin' your time. For bringin' you all this way for nothin'. A total waste of bloody time."

Ill-tempered shopping-traffic snarled us as we made our way north out of Cork city. I clicked the windscreen wiper stalk to intermittent to ease the squeal of rubber on glass.

"You did well," Paul said. "Thanks. Gave them both a thorough interrogation. Done that type of thing before?"

I was pleased with my performance in the meeting. Something about Ireland made it easier to meet people, easier to talk to, and at, strangers. My confidence had grown. An old younger-self returning? I felt at home, rooted. Unlike Paul. Ireland felt familiar. Ireland was therapy.

Paul had presented his birth certificate and passport to Dr Fitzpatrick and Sister Agnes Brown. They claimed the birth certificate was evidence he wasn't born at the Home, or even in Cork. What he tried to argue might be an administrative error, they argued was fact. He was deflated. I wanted him to say more, encouraged him, expected it, but he shrunk into himself, crossing his legs and rattling his tea cup when he returned it to its saucer.

"I've sat in on a few police interviews," I said. "Escorting prisoners, that sort of thing. But did you notice the hair flicks, and the hands to the face? Classic signs. They're covering something up, alright."

We nodded in affirmation. A green light. I edged the car forward a few more feet, we weren't moving far.

"How do you feel about what they told us?" I asked.

Paul was pensive.

A gap opened up in the traffic. The lights turned red, but I drove the car over the junction into the space. A red Ford Fiesta with Dublin registration plates sounded its horn.

"To tell the truth, right now it feels bloody hopeless," Paul said at last. "Either they say they've no records goin' back far enough, or that they can't break confidentiality. It's me I want to know about. It's my confidentiality."

The red Fiesta revved its engine behind us, windscreen wipers waving us out of the way.

"Couldn't have done much searchin'," Paul said. "Through the records I mean. We first called the Centre four days ago. I just wonder how hard they looked."

We were stationary. The Fiesta filled my mirrors. The driver's arm shot across his chest to unclasp his seatbelt. He opened his door. A booted ankle appeared on the road.

The traffic ahead moved clear. The engine hummed as we accelerated away.

"And like you," Paul continued, "I didn't buy that 'neither of us worked here at the time' excuse. That's just bloody lame. And I was delighted when you told them as much."

"Paul, I know yesterday, with a few pints inside us, I said different, but there's a distinct possibility that we won't find your mother at all. You realise that, don't you?"

He tutted.

I clicked on the blower switch to clear mist from the windscreen and cool the atmosphere in the car. "We're up against the authorities with this," I said. "And against these Homes. Even the Church. After that meeting, I've a bad feeling, and if what I think went on in these Mother and Baby Homes *did* go on, they'll all be closing ranks." I'd volunteered too much.

Paul pushed back in his seat.

The traffic moved freely. A sign with a vertical white arrow said, 'N20 *Luimneach* Limerick'. I relaxed a little when the red Ford Fiesta turned left behind us.

"So what do *you* think went on?"

I thought about reaching for the radio knob. "Worst-case scenario, okay? Probably didn't happen at all, but let's take the worst case."

"Go on," Paul said with reluctant curiosity.

"Your birth mother gets pregnant by some horny lothario."

"Mmm."

I regretted my description of his birth father but continued. "Is sent away to have her baby. To avoid the shame, or whatever, to one of the Homes. Baby born. You, in this case. Baby adopted out to a childless couple for a fee."

"For a fee?"

"Hold on–"

"You sayin' my parents bought me? Like a new bloody car? Turned up at one of these Homes and said 'We'll take him, the one with zero miles on the clock and a clean set of tyres. Here's a hundred dollars'. Shit 'n' strewth."

His naivety astounded me. "I'm only compiling a worst-case scenario."

Paul glared at the road ahead and blew out through tight lips.

I continued. "I'm thinking it might explain the reluctance to be forthcoming with the records. Or the reluctance to even search for the records. That Dr Fitzpatrick was very coy about there being any records at all, but I don't believe that for a minute. They might be sparse, and they may not be the records we need, but there would be records. Even if they were only accounting records. Someone in authority would want to know how much was being paid for the children."

"Jeez, you make it sound so bloody sordid. Was that legal?"

"To sell children? I doubt it."

"Jesus H. Christ."

We drove on in silence, through drizzle, towards Limerick.

34

Andrea left without making comment. Her chair whirred her out of the kitchen.

"I didn't fare much better," Niamh said watching her mother go. "Father Donal was insistent on us not involving old Father Brendan, and the other Homes on our hit list have all closed down. No-one's answering the phone except St Clare's in Meath, and that's now a home for the elderly. They said they were unable to help us but we were welcome to call in on them for a drop of tea. I did, however, contact Nora Lacey again."

"Have I heard that name?" Paul said. "Sounds vaguely familiar."

"The woman from County Hall. The one who compiled the list for us."

"I remember. And?"

"She couldn't help with more Home names, but we got talking and after a while she told me something that she asked us not to repeat."

Paul shifted on his chair.

"She swore me to secrecy." Niamh waited for our nods of compliance. "She has a cousin, up in Dublin, and he knows someone, who knows someone else, who works for An Bord Uchtála. A friend-of-a-friend sort of thing." She smiled at our blank faces. "An Bord Uchtála? The Adoption Board. You'd think ye lads'd learn to speak the language before ye come over to Ireland ... Anyway, Nora was on the phone to the cousin fella, arranging a visit to Sligo or something, when she happened to mention about us going into County Hall. Didn't the cousin tell her about this friend-of-a-friend who reckons there are calls for a wholescale Government investigation into the adoptions carried out in Mother and Baby Homes." She turned to Paul. "In the forties and fifties, Paul. Your era."

"Why?" Paul said. He scraped his chair closer to the table and wrapped his large hands around his mug of tea. "What're they investigatin'?"

"She didn't know. Just said that it's all very hush-hush, very secretive. The government is under pressure to launch an enquiry and for the Minister of State for Children to lead the investigation." Niamh lifted her head and peered through the half-moon of her spectacles to consult a note. "A Mr Frank Faley."

"Blimey," Paul said. "Gets more and more worryin'

"Her cousin thinks nothing will come of it," Niamh said. "Says there're too many obstacles to overcome and probably too many important people with reputations at stake. Thinks it'll be made out to be a fuss about nothing."

"When's the cousin comin' to Sligo?" Paul asked. "Can we meet him?"

"Not for another two months. You'll be the other side of the world by then."

Paul winced and sighed and gazed down into the depths of his black tea.

"What did Father Donal Kealey say?" I asked Niamh.

"He won't allow us to bother Father Brendan. Says he's too ill and too old to remember anything."

"Still says an open mass most weeks," I said.

"Who?" Niamh said. "Father Brendan Kealey? He's a hundred and fifty years old if he's a day. He'll have retired, surely."

"Stumbles a bit, according to your Father Donal. And substitutes his own words into the Lord's Prayer when he's unsure. But priests never retire. You a practising Catholic, Paul?"

Paul blushed.

"About time you went to mass again," I said.

35

I never had the courage to sit near Mary at mass on Sundays, fearful her mother, vigilant beside her, would throttle me with her rosary beads if I ever came close. So I sat with the men at the back of the church, talking in hushed tones about farming, football and fair days. When the volume of conversation impinged on Father Brendan Kealey's homily, he called us out.

"And what is it you men have to say to each other that is more important than the words of God?"

His bellow halted us.

If the interruption occurred after the monetary offerings the curmudgeonly Father Brendan would let rip with, "If ye've no intention of listening to God's mass, let ye not bother staying."

Wives turned and tutted at their husbands.

Husbands blushed and hushed up. None walked.

The nearest I'd get to Mary would be passing the end of her pew with a collection basket. I'd hand in the basket and await its return the next pew forward, all the time staring at Mary. I'd note where she touched the rim of the basket. When it came back to me I'd hold it in the same spot.

Mary wouldn't risk alerting her mother by looking at me. And I carried on pretending her mother didn't notice.

The other collectors and I performed a small ritual at the front of the church when we handed over the alms. Old Timmy Ryan poured the coins from our baskets into his and stacked the empties underneath. We all bowed together, and Mr Ryan handed the stack of baskets to the priest with a look that suggested he had donated every penny himself. Ignoring the rest of us Father Kealey would thank Mr Ryan with a bow and hand the baskets to James Burke.

I often thought about plunging my arm into the mass of money and making off with a handful of coin for my mother. I know for a fact that James Burke used to dip discreetly as he placed the pillar of baskets at the back of the altar. James kept it to a penny a mass, too smart to risk discovery from jingling coins and losing the altar boy job. He also admitted severe reservations about being condemned to eternal damnation by an uncompromising Father Kealey.

I'd spy Mary out as I walked back down the aisle to the rear of the church. She'd fix her eyes on the pew in front of her, determined not to look up.

"Were ya scared I'd say hello in mass?" I'd tease her when we'd meet. "Yer mammy there."

"No," she'd say and walk ahead.

I'd laugh. "You were scared." I'd catch her up. "Why didn't ya look?"

"Why *did* you look?" she'd say, nudging a shoulder into me.

"Because yer lovely to look at."

36

"Do I know ya, I don't?"

The handrail saved the white-haired woman from toppling when she leaned back to look up at Paul. Her accent took me back to the beach and Mary's imitation of her mother.

"Don't worry about that, my lovely. Seen you waitin'. Grab this arm if you need it."

"If I walk into the church linked to you, they'll think I'm weddin' meself a new fancy man."

Niamh smiled and winked.

"When she took ill, my mother disliked steps too," Paul said.

"Your mother? You're well trained so. I don't like when people just grab a hold o' me."

"My mother preferred to hold on."

"And I prefer to hold on."

Niamh and I followed Paul and the woman up the concrete steps, the woman clearly regarding herself too capable to walk the less-demanding access slope.

We entered the chapel, appended to the south side of the main nursing home building, through a nondescript doorway. Niamh and I found our own seats. The woman introduced her 'fancy man' to her friends in whispered greetings, not letting go his arm.

Paul nodded and shook everyone's hand before striding down the side of the church to join us. His pace quickened and his smile dissolved with each step, as though recalling the serious intent of his visit. It was interesting to see this otherwise confident, successful man wither in such circumstances.

The chapel was light and airy, with high magnolia walls. A waft of new paint blew through the aisles with each opening of the door. A stained-glass window image of Christ on a cross splashed red and blue and yellow light over the congregation.

The peace of the chapel calmed me. My limbs fell loose, my muscles slack. Paul fidgeted beside me, a knee bouncing.

A young nun spotted us, gathered together three missals, and floated over. "I'm Sister Joan," she said. "Welcome to St Martin's Nursing Home. Will you all be taking communion?"

"Yes please, Sister," Niamh said.

"No," I said. "Thank you, though."

Paul examined his fingers.

After a brief pause, Sister Joan displayed a conspicuous set of teeth and said, "I'll count it as two, then." She handed me the missals.

An elderly nun tapped Sister Joan on the shoulder and whispered into her ear. Sister Joan turned back to us and smiled her teeth. "Excuse me, I've to help Father Brendan to the altar. Enjoy the service."

"Sister, before you go," Niamh said standing up and leaning over me. "Do you think we could meet with Father Brendan after mass?"

Sister Joan's eyes flicked over each of us and back to Niamh. "Are you close friends of Father Brendan, or family?"

"No," Niamh said, shaking her head. "No, we're not. We'd just like to have a chat with him."

"Is he expecting you?"

"No. No, we just hoped to catch him after mass. My uncle knew him as a child."

"I don't mind asking him, then," Sister Joan said. "And I'll check with the Operations Manager." She hurried away.

The pews were full to capacity. Ambulant residents occupied the central positions. Residents in wheelchairs and residents supported by frames and those chaperoned by carers in pale-blue uniforms occupied the ends of the bench seats. At least a dozen nuns, all dressed in cardigans and navy-blue veils over white coifs, dotted the congregation.

Sister Joan wheeled the chair through a door at the side of the altar prompting those in the congregation that could to rise to their feet. She leaned into the push as they ascended a small wooden ramp. Behind her a nun pulled a black and white cylinder of oxygen on a yellow metal trolley. Sister Joan parked the priest behind a microphone stand.

His head was drooped, his chin on his chest. A nasal cannula ran under a bulging nose, the plastic tube pressing into liver-spotted cheeks before looping over large ears. The neat, white hair reflected a blue stain from the window behind him. His long frame curled in the chair beneath generous folds of peach liturgical vestments.

Sister Joan adjusted the position of the microphone.

Father Brendan Kealey transported me to a Templeboy of forty years earlier as he made the sign of the cross with a trembling hand, and his frail but familiar amplified voice reached us through speakers on the walls. "In the name o' the Father ... And o' the Son ... And o' the Holy Ghost ..."

"I've spoken to Mrs Coyle, the Operations Manager," Sister Joan said. "And she suggests that as Father Brendan is now resting after saying mass, it might be best if you make an appointment to come back another time. I'm sorry." The toothy smile.

We had relocated to a pew at the front of the empty chapel.

"We only want to speak with him a short while," Niamh said. "Five minutes, only."

"I'm sorry," Sister Joan said, wringing her hands. "Father Brendan doesn't receive many visitors, you see. He would need to be well rested and ready to meet you. If you telephoned the Home with a request to visit, it would be arranged. I'm sorry."

Niamh said, "I'll bet you he only ever receives the one visitor, am I right?"

Sister Joan squinted. "I'm sorry, I'm really not at liberty to–"

"Father Donal Kealey?" Niamh said.

The nun hid the teeth but allowed the eyes to smile. A blush rose in her cheeks.

Niamh took half a step forward and whispered, "Don't *you* think they're father and son? I'm convinced of it. Both so handsome."

Sister Joan rocked back and filled the chapel with nervous laughter. She covered her mouth, but the smile peeked around her fingers.

"Thank you for letting us stay for the mass," Paul said in his rising-tone voice. "We'll make an appointment."

37

Niamh strode into the kitchen. "Bloody hell, I didn't know priests were allowed to swear like that. I thought all that cursing was knocked out of them with a stiff rod at the seminary. Mrs Coyle wasn't long reporting us to Father Donal. He was angry as hell." She turned to me and pointed. "Angry at us, but he's really mad with you."

"That was him on the phone, right?" Paul said.

"Said he told you to leave Father Brendan out of this." Niamh traipsed around the kitchen, wagging a finger at me. "Said he warned you about his health. Said you've deliberately gone against his wishes. And he said you're going to rot in purgatory for all eternity."

Paul grinned. "Purgatory?"

"Not really," Niamh said. "He didn't say that last bit. He's too lovely for that. But I think he's of a mind to hold the three of us there if he could."

Paul asked, "Did you tell him we're going to make an appointment?"

"I did, and he said he wants to be there."

"All four of us?"

"No, one of us," Niamh said. "And him. He said four would be too many. Something about the last time Father Brendan had four visitors would be back in nineteen-eighty-one when the Bishop called to congratulate him on sixty years in the priesthood. Four now would likely cause a stroke. I really do like Father Donal, he's funny even when he doesn't mean to be."

I said, "Paul, you need to go."

Paul sat back in his chair and reflected. "Not really. I think you'd be better. This could be our only chance of a breakthrough and there's half a chance he'll remember you."

"I agree with Paul," Niamh said, lining up mugs on the kitchen table to receive tea. "You'd know what to ask. Pretend you're interrogating a prisoner."

"I didn't interrogate prisoners."

"You can discuss old times," Paul said. "Drag the old memories out of him. We need to let Andrea know what we're doing."

"I'll wake Mammy now for some tea. She doesn't seem at her best lately."

"I'm goin' for a run before I eat." Paul pushed back his chair. "Steady my nerves."

"We talked," Niamh said when Paul left. "He's despondent again."

"I know."

"He's so desperate, when we were at the mass he was looking around to see if he'd recognise his mother in the congregation."

"I hope we find something out from old Father Brendan."

"You need to make sure you do," Niamh said.

38

I didn't notice her until she was beside us.

"I'm Mrs Coyle," she said looking down on me. "The Operations Manager here at St Martin's. You're both very welcome. How are you keeping, Father Donal?"

Father Donal and I rocked ourselves out of low, soft-sponged chairs to stand.

Sister Joan appeared behind the reception desk and occupied herself inspecting the visitor book and shuffling paper.

"Busy, Orla, busy," Father Donal said. "I like what you've done to the décor, it's given the place a lift. You've clearly been busy here too."

"Oh, it needed it, Father, it needed it. I think you'll be delighted with the chapel. It feels beautifully light and airy."

I nodded in agreement.

Orla Coyle dismissed my opinion with a sour-mouthed sideways glance. "If you'll both follow me, I'll bring you through."

As we moved away, Father Donal gave a nonchalant wave of his hat in the direction of the reception desk.

We followed the plump Operations Manager along a wide, cushion-floored corridor and pushed through swing doors into a large communal area. An arc of high-backed chairs sat empty. I could smell boiled bacon, urine-stained upholstery and wallpaper paste, plus a distinct undertone of dying flesh reminiscent of my father's leg.

"Lunch is just finishing," Mrs Coyle said, presumably to explain the empty chairs.

We passed along another corridor of calming pale-green walls and light-pine doors and stopped outside door number 12.

A small wooden crucifix hung nailed to the door above the plastic numerals. I thought of Jesus and his apostles, the room choice appropriate.

Mrs Coyle knocked and entered.

A care assistant wearing a white plastic apron dabbed at the mouth of Father Brendan Kealey. She straightened as we entered. "We've just finished. I'll take the plate tray and be out yer way." Then louder, "I'll be seeing you later, Father Brendan. To collect you for the bingo this evening." She untied a bib from around his neck. "Do you want me to turn the heating down …? No …? You're alright, are ya?"

"Thank you, Bridie," Mrs Coyle said.

Bridie flapped a hand in front of her face and puffed out air. She checked the vial reading on the oxygen concentrator pump before manoeuvring her tray through the door.

Father Brendan sat hunched in a winged chair beside a neatly dressed bed. The bed was draped in an orange camberwick bedspread, the swirl of the tufts shaped like a bishop's mitre. A crucifix, identical to the one on the door, was fixed to the wall above the centre of his pillows.

Father Brendan looked shrunken. The bones of his shoulders pushed through a beige crimplene cardigan that gathered on his lap. Veined hands rested on the folds, his withered fingers woven together. He stared down on them, his head swaying on the end of a bent, scrawny neck. A decrepit relic of his former intimidating self.

His breath was more laboured than it had been two days earlier when he celebrated mass in the chapel. He even looked less familiar, the close-up detail magnifying his deterioration. The skin over his high cheek bones was stretched as thin as a coat of magnolia on the chapel walls. His nose and ears looked engorged, with curled grey strands of hair leaping from the dark orifices. Though splashed with flat brown patches, the face retained remnants of the handsomeness I remembered from my youth. The fine white hair was clean and well-trimmed.

The concentrator pump hissed with each inhalation, delivering clean oxygen to his nostrils.

We settled in two chairs pulled up close in front of the elderly priest.

"I'll leave you to it," Mrs Coyle said. "Father Donal, can you please remind our visitor to sign out when he leaves? We'll speak soon."

"Of course."

We sat in silence and watched Father Brendan breathe, unsure who should speak first.

Father Brendan said, "Who's this man?" The voice was slow and gurgling, as though bubbling through water. His head remained bent over, facing into his lap.

Father Donal shuffled closer. "Hello, Father Brendan. This is an old friend from Templeboy. Would you know him?"

Half a minute passed. With a small gasp of effort Father Brendan leaned back in his chair. Pale-blue rheumy eyes in hollow sockets surveyed me. His eyelids were heavy, giving him the look of a sad and frightened Basset puppy. The cannula bobbed below his nose as he pursed and pulled his lips. The deep, rounded crevice of his chin held a smear of gravy. There was no flicker of recognition. He leaned forward again. "I know 'im."

"You do?" Father Donal barked a small laugh and slapped me on the arm.

"And I knew the father," Father Brendan rasped, his head nodding. "A proper good-for-feck-all."

The oxygen pump hissed, refilling the elderly priest's airways.

Father Donal shifted in his seat and inhaled through a smile. He said, "I'm sure he did the best he could for his family."

I knew what was coming.

"A drunk!" Father Brendan's voice was clear, no gurgling, no bubbling.

The pump hissed.

I removed my jacket and leaned towards him. "I wanted to ask if you remember any girl from Sligo town being sent away to a Mother and Baby Home. In the late nineteen-fifties."

Father Brendan sat still in his chair.

"Can you remember?" Father Donal said. And then to me, "He can't remember." Louder again, "It was too long ago."

"Nineteen-fifty-eight," I said. "The year after my father lost the leg."

I pulled at the collar of my shirt and wiped beads of sweat from my forehead. A picture of the Sacred Heart of Jesus gazed down on me from the wall behind the elderly priest's head, pleading for forbearance. "She got pregnant," I said. "Very young. Unmarried. Probably sent away to have the baby. Thought you might know of her."

The pump pushed more oxygen into Father Brendan.

"There's a man," I continued. "Her son. Came over all the way from Australia."

"He doesn't remember," Father Donal said.

"He was adopted to Australia," I said, louder. "His name is Paul McDonnell. Doesn't know who his own mother is. He's here now, looking for her." Louder still, "The mother's from Sligo town. Nineteen-fifty-eight."

"He doesn't remember," Father Donal repeated.

"He might," I said. "He hasn't met me in almost forty years and he remembered me."

"He was always good with faces."

"The girl was sent away," I said to the white-topped head. "Maybe only sixteen or seventeen years old."

Father Donal shifted to the edge of his seat.

I continued. "Sent to a Mother and Baby Home. From Sligo town. Nineteen-fifty-eight."

Father Donal placed his hand on my arm. "I don't think—"

"Probably had the child adopted and taken away against the young girl's wishes."

Father Donal grasped my shirt sleeve. "Stop."

126

"Did you know the girl?" I said, almost shouting. "Paul McDonnell wants to know. As Parish Priest, you would have known about it. You would have sanctioned it. You would have sent her away."

"Enough." Father Donal tugged my arm. "Show some respect for God's sake. He's an elderly gentleman. He doesn't remember."

I pulled my arm free and slumped in the seat. I pushed back my hair and rubbed at the damp nape of my neck. Father Brendan Kealy said nothing. The visit had been a waste of time. I felt frustrated for Paul. The elderly priest knew nothing. I regretted shouting.

The lengths of clear plastic tubing taped together behind Father Brendan stirred. The white head shook. The pump hissed.

"No," Father Brendan said, his head bobbing.

Father Donal said, "We'd better go. He clearly can't remember and he's getting upset"

"No," Father Brendan croaked. "No." A solitary drop of clear liquid splashed the top finger of his clasped hands.

"Is he crying?" I asked. "He remembers something."

"You're upsetting him. We must go, now." Father Donal reached for the red pull-cord hanging from the ceiling and tugged. Nothing happened. "We must leave."

I didn't want to leave. I studied Father Brendan, looking for clues, reading the language of his body, ready to push and probe like the police investigators I observed in interviews. I chose to wait, deploying silence. Would he fill the void? The guilty always fill a void, patch the hole with information they didn't want to reveal. Rapid knocks on the door distracted us.

Sister Joan entered, her neat eyebrows drawn together beneath the edge of her starched coif, and strode towards us.

"Sister Joan," Father Donal said and stood, running the rim of his hat through his fingers. "He's got a bit upset, I'm afraid.

It's my fault, I'm sorry. We're about to leave. I didn't want him to be alone when he's like this."

Sister Joan checked the vial gauge.

I rose and stepped clear to let her kneel beside the whimpering priest.

"What caused this?" she asked stroking his white hair.

"It's my fault," Father Donal said. "I shouldn't have allowed this to happen. We'll go, let you care for him. God bless, Sister Joan."

She raised herself to her full height and turned. "Is this why you wanted to meet Father Brendan after Sunday mass?" She stood between me and the elderly Father Brendan, shielding him. "Is it? So you could upset him like this? May God forgive you."

"I–"

"Sister." Father Donal's voice was soft, his tone familiar. He placed a hand on her fist. The fist eased open. Their fingers hesitated before interlacing, wary in my presence. "I'll deal with him." Then to me, "Come on, we must go."

In the corridor, a triangular lamp located above door 12 flashed red light over the pale-green walls. The oppressive heat and the intermittent splash of ochre turned my stomach.

Care Assistant Bridie rushed towards us, red flashes reflecting on her pale, freckled face.

Father Donal Kealey and I walked back to the reception area, through a fermented smell of renovation, cooked food and ammonia.

39

"Mammy's not great, now," Niamh said. "The doctor called in on his way home from the surgery and he's given her something to settle her for the night. She'll be fine in the morning, th'elp o' God."

Paul pressed the rocker switch on the electric kettle. The kettle rasped into life and got to work warming water. "So we're no further forward," he said. "I'm down to my last few days and we're no further forward. I'm running out of time. I need to return to Australia and … I'm not goin' to find her, am I?"

Niamh rattled cupboard doors, looking for mugs.

I peered into my nightcap glass of whiskey.

"You won't find your mother," Niamh said. "But you have met me and Mammy, so the journey's not completely wasted." She dangled a mug from a finger and sashayed around Paul.

He blushed and smiled at her.

"I still maintain there's mileage in old Brendan Kealey," I said. "Something registered with him."

"First, you make him cry," Niamh said. "And now you're not even giving him his full title. He's a priest. Shame on you."

"You should have heard the language out of him," I said. "Will you go and see Father Donal again, Niamh?"

"No need," she said leaning over the sink to peer out of the window. "The gorgeous delight-in-a-dog-collar is here himself, now."

"He's here?" Paul said. He moved to the window to glimpse out, and then rushed to sit down opposite me like a mischievous inmate told the guard is coming.

We listened to Niamh's greeting at the front door.

She flounced back into the kitchen just as the thump and bash of the kettle clicked off. "I'm sad to announce, Father Donal Kealey is here for you." She swooped an arm in my direction. "And not me." The grandiose gesture drew another smile from Paul.

A hatted Father Donal followed Niamh in. He didn't intend staying. "Have you a few minutes, please?" he said to me. "It concerns Father Brendan."

"Is he alright?" I asked.

"I was called back into St Martin's again. A phone call late this afternoon. I'm not long back from Sligo. There's something I need to tell you, personally. Alone, if you don't mind."

40

Outside the back door, caught in a fleeting rectangle of kitchen light, the black and orange and white cat in the outlaw's eye-mask presided over a twitching field mouse at its feet.

I pulled closed the door and followed the young priest towards the old barn, fastening my coat against the chill. I glanced back at Niamh and Paul, silhouetted in the kitchen window looking out.

A motion detector clicked in the darkness and the yard flooded with light. A windfall of cherry-tree blossom littered the ground like pink snow. Lichen and moss patched the gapped stonework of the barn. A rusty, flattened nail hook I remembered from childhood stuck out at head height, its utility long lost, its purpose long forgotten.

Father Donal took a packet of cigarettes from his pocket.

"Thought you were kicking the habit?" I said.

"I am," he said. "First in almost a week. Extreme circumstances. Do you?" He offered me the packet.

"I have another vice," I said.

"Inherited from the father?" He stared. "I'm sorry, that was unnecessary." He waited for me to accept his apology, to grant him absolution.

I didn't.

He lit his cigarette with a tremor, sucked on it noisily and blew grey smoke into the light. "You know Sister Joan from the Nursing Home, don't you?"

Of course I did. "I do," I said. "But not as well as you."

He paused his cigarette, wedged between two rigid fingers, in front of his lips. An awkward smoker, he lacked the elegance of the experienced addict.

"I'm sorry, that was unnecessary," I said.

The face behind the curling smoke smiled, the shadow of his hat rim stretching his features.

"You warned them at the home to expect us, didn't you?" I said. "Told them to send us away if we turned up without you."

"I needed to protect Father Brendan," he said.

"I can see this isn't easy, so please, just tell me, has something happened to him?"

"As an author," he said, "you'll have read James Joyce?"

A tingle of embarrassment climbed the back of my neck. Write a book and everyone expects you to have read everything ever printed. Why didn't he ask about Steinbeck? "*Portrait of an Artist*," I said, relieved I could recall a title.

"A *Portrait of* the *Artist*," he corrected. "*As a Young Man*. I didn't really get on with it, thought it far too—"

"Father Donal, you said you had something to tell me."

"Yes, sorry. It's just that Joyce made use of epiphanies. So-called Joycean epiphany? He used epiphanies as a literary device in *Dubliners*. Something would happen to the characters in each of the stories that would cause them to realise something pertinent about themselves. And that realisation would alter their whole perception of who they were, what they were—"

"I'm familiar with the literary device." I lied.

The end of his cigarette glowed when he inhaled. He drew down his thin brows beneath the rim of his hat. He looked like a cowboy. "You caused Father Brendan to have an epiphany of sorts earlier this afternoon," he said, and blew a plume from his nose. He was remembering how to smoke.

I said, "What do you want to tell me?"

"Sister Joan, whom you know, called a couple of hours after we left. Father Brendan asked for me to come back into the Home. I went straight in. He told me everything. It wasn't a confession, more an unburdening, but it *was* like an epiphany. And because it wasn't a confession, I can share it with you now."

"So he hasn't died, then?"

"No. He's probably on his way back from playing bingo as we speak."

"Thank God for that," I said.

"Indeed." He smiled briefly. "But you need to understand that what I'm about to tell you could have wide ramifications. Especially if you started writing about it in some serialised novel, for example. I want to share it with you, you deserve to know. I believe your family deserves to know. But you have to swear to me that you will contain what I say within your own family for the time being."

"Jesus, what is it you're going to say?"

He let the statement pass and took a last draw of smoke. He quenched the tip in a gap in the barn wall, blowing smoke over his fingers as he crumpled the cigarette. "You have to swear."

"I can't guarantee I can contain anything. My family are adults, they make up their own—"

"To the best of your ability. Promise me you'll contain it to the best of your ability, they'll listen to you. It needn't be forever, Father Brendan's not long for this world but I must protect him. Only weeks left according to the doctors."

I stared at the young priest in the hat. He looked solemn, genuine, full of grace. I wished I knew how to smoke. I wished I didn't drink. I needed a drink. I didn't want to hear what he was about to tell me. "Fine."

"As we're not in a confessional, we'll shake hands instead."

We shook, his grip overly firm, nervy.

He leaned his back against the wall and pulled the cigarette packet from his pocket. "It's those two in the window I'm most worried about."

I studied the house while he struck a match.

"Father Brendan didn't lie to you when he said he didn't remember a girl from Sligo being sent away to a Mother and Baby Home … It wasn't one girl he remembers. It's two. And they weren't from Sligo town." Father Donal jerked his back away from the wall and leaned his shoulder against it to face me. Smoke coiled around the visible white edge of his clerical collar and up to the flat of his fedora.

I thought then that this man's sermons at mass on Sundays would be worth listening to. He could hold an audience.

"They came from here," he said. "From Templeboy."

Templeboy? I came from Templeboy. Why didn't I know them? The place wasn't so big that I wouldn't know two girls sent off to a Home to have babies. "I know these two girls, don't I? Is one of them Paul's mother?"

He nodded. "Yes. Remember you swore to contain this."

My stomach fluttered, my heart hammered my ribs.

"The two girls were with child," he said. "They were both unmarried. They were both very young. And they were sent away to a Home together."

I whispered, "Tell me their names."

"Andrea McCabe."

"Andrea?!"

"And Mary O'Brien."

My legs faltered.

Father Donal grabbed the lapels of my coat and held me against the wall.

"Mary?" I gasped. I smelled of burning fabric.

"Oh, Jesus!" Father Donal patted away the cigarette end. "I've burnt a hole in your coat. I'm sorry"

I leaned forward as he backed away, propped on my knees, and gulped singed air.

"You alright?" he asked.

I didn't reply. I didn't have an answer. Only questions. Mary? My child? Sisters of Mercy? Not my Mary? Answers came to me. Yes, Mary. Her mother's scorn for me. Her uncle's cabin. The dry, midge-ridden August of 1957. Dublin? Unlikely, could be anywhere. Is Paul my son? How much did old Father Brendan Kealey know? Did he know if Paul McDonnell was my son?

"What else did he tell you?" I said, my breathing recovered. I remained propped over.

"Paul's not your son," Father Donal said.

I scrunched my face. Disappointment? Relief? All of it.

"By all accounts, Mary lost the child ... I'm sorry."

What happened to Mary in the Mother and Baby Home to prevent her having more children? What hell did she go through? I cried. For our child. I cried for Mary, for her want of a child, for her need of a child, for the gaping, child-shaped hole in her life, in my life. For what we could have had. For what was ours. Mine and Mary's. "The child was mine."

"I'm so sorry," Father Donal said.

I felt his hand on my back.

"Father Brendan visited the girls," he said. "Andrea gave birth to a baby boy. Father Brendan helped choose the adoptive parents, Mr and Mrs McDonnell. Good Catholics, living in London, about to move to Sydney. He even suggested the name. Paul the Apostle held his faith in God and in Jesus Christ way above any respect he might have had for the law. It was the perfect name."

I snorted back snot and wiped my face with a sleeve, lifted my back to the wall and blew air out into the floodlit night. Addled moths, drunk on light, thumped against the hot glass of the lamp.

"Paul's father," I said. "It can't be Sean. Do we know?"

"Paul's father died with your brother, on a motorbike. Patrick Layden, you may have known him, I think you were in the same class at school. They were both killed by a drunk driver on the Sligo Road."

"My God." A double funeral. Four years ago. The funeral I was too drunk to come home for. "Our child?" I asked. "What do you know of our child?"

"A baby girl. Stillborn from all accounts. Apparently, buried at the Home."

I rubbed the back of my hand into my forehead and slid it back over my hair. A fuzziness. Familiar, unwanted. Breathe.

"From what I hear, the birth was … Difficult. Mary went through a heap of trauma."

Blood throbbed at my temples. I closed my eyes and pictured Mary, tear-streaked, bloodied and sweating, reaching for our daughter. My daughter. Our dead daughter. I pushed the image away. Something was not quite right. "You said 'apparently'. How does Father Brendan know where the baby was buried? Did he say how he knew? Why wasn't she buried here?"

"He was told. He was told the baby was stillborn and removed from the mother immediately. For the mother's sake … 'What the eye doesn't see, the heart doesn't grieve for' … It was the way of it back then."

"Did Mary see the child at all? Did she hold her?" I asked.

"I … I don't know. Father Brendan implied not. But you can ask her yourself."

"Does she know you're telling me all this?"

"I just came from her house. I've to return there, her husband has come home to die. I don't know if it's best you come with me or not."

"Mary gave you permission to tell me?" I asked.

"Mary and Andrea … She and Andrea spoke about this only a few days ago, they both want you and Paul to know the truth. There's a concern, however. They think Paul and Niamh have become too close. And, it seems, Andrea is not taking the whole situation too well. That's what's caused the delay in the telling. The doctor called to Andrea this evening."

I nodded.

Father Donal extracted another cigarette from the packet with his teeth. He had more to say. He bent his head to cupped hands. When he straightened, the tip of the cigarette flared red and his eyes blinked rapidly in the shadow of the fedora rim. He let smoke fill his lungs, took the cigarette between thumb and two fingers sheltering it in the curl of his hand, and squinted.

Like the Marlboro Man but more nervous. Smoking had come back to him.

"What is it?" I asked.

"It was in Tuam. Galway. The Mother and Baby Home was in Tuam."

Closed now I remembered. Early sixties according to Paul. "Not Sligo?"

"Not Sligo, no," he said. "I think Mary had relations in Tuam, an aunt I think, so it made sense. But listen, there are some worrying rumours about Tuam, and this is where the story gets … I'm afraid there's talk of a *lot* of recorded stillbirths at the Tuam Home."

"Incompetent bastards."

"Or judiciously expedient."

"I don't under–"

"This is mostly rumour." He pointed a finger of his cigarette hand at me. "And remember you swore to contain this."

The end of his cigarette glowed like the lamp of a lighthouse warning of peril in the night. I felt I was about to crash upon its rocks. "What is it?"

"Mary has a certificate of death for your daughter," he said. "But there is a chance your daughter may still be alive."

I groaned at the lightning pain that burned across the front of my head. Metallic taste. I knew where this led. Synapses misfired. Neural connections collapsed. Confusion. The floodlight clicked off, disorientating blackness, and flashed back on. My vision blurred. I fell in and out of semi-consciousness. The main house, Niamh and Paul a haze in the blazing light of the window, rotated and rushed towards me. I clamped my eyes closed as it crushed me against the rough stonework of the barn.

My eyes opened. Harold Vinceman had me against the prison cell wall. His arm, bloody from angry self-inflicted cuts, pressed across my throat, choking off my breath. A triangle-tipped blade flashed ruby-red in front of my face. Vinceman told me what he was going to do to me. "I'm going to bleed you like halal." His accomplices cackled either side of him and pinned my shoulders back. I could smell their sweat.

I flailed at the muscled arm, pathetic attempts to enact ineffective training. The arm pressed harder, crushing my windpipe. I felt the point of the blade press my throat, the pain sharp, intense. Vinceman sneered. I found a breath and cried out, twisting my neck. I closed my eyes to die.

Father Donal shouted, "It's alright, I've got you!"

I forced open my eyes.

Father Donal, cigarette dangling crooked from the side of his mouth, hat dislodged and resting over an ear, held me up against the stonework. "It's alright," he said, his voice rapid. "Breathe easy, I have you."

"Away from me," I gasped. My head burned between my temples. I blinked hot eyes.

Father Donal held me. "You passed out, can you stand?"

"I'm fine … Please." I eased his hands away. "I'm fine." The pain in my skull roared flames. I inhaled deeply, as the head-woman taught me. "When it happens," she said, "use all your senses. Stay in the present." The cool evening air dampened the fire. I smelled the darkness, the salt from the sea, I was alive. I didn't want to hear any more. I wanted to hear more. I wanted to hear everything. "Explain it to me like you would a child."

He raised his arms as he backed away and straightened his fedora. "Perhaps I've said enough."

"No. No, you must go on … Please." I rubbed a hand against my throat. "They're just flashbacks. It's not the first time."

"Flashbacks? To what? Do you remember shouting?"

"What did I shout?"

"You screamed for Mary. Frightened the life out of me. Look, don't you think we should go back into the house? We'll continue this again."

It was Mary that saved me the first time. "Mary?" Vinceman laughed. "Did he just fuckin' call me Mary?" Six seconds. Time enough for the prison guards to open the door and pounce.

I shook my head. "No. Please tell me. I must know."

Father Donal sucked hard on the bent cigarette. "Alright, so. Alright. If you're sure." He shuffled from side to side, crushing blossom. "There's been talk. For a long time. Rumours about the Mother and Baby Home in Tuam. About the high number of deaths at birth. It's thought the number was *too* high, even for an incompetent maternity unit. There have been allegations." He examined the cigarette, weighing it in his hand, and decided to take another pull. He held the smoke and blurted, "It's thought some of the babies didn't die at all but were sold to couples from overseas."

I gasped. "What? That's ... Isn't that trafficking? Some sick form of black market in babies? There'd be certificates, no?"

"A falsified death certificate could be drawn up and retained here. The death certificate would satisfy the authorities. No questions would be asked."

"How did they get away with that?"

He squirmed his neck beneath his crisp collar. "Think," he said. "What are the two most powerful institutions in the country?"

I didn't have to answer, but the words fell out of my mouth. "State and Church."

"You must remember that adoption, regulated or not, was, and continues to be, seen as an act of compassion. Adoption provides a safe and compassionate home for bastard babies. The just and the righteous compensating for the sins of the mothers."

"There'll be graves," I said. "There'll be marked graves for the babies that died."

"No."

"What do you mean, 'no'?"

He dropped the cigarette to the blossom. "There was a confidential ecclesiastical report about Tuam." He stared me in the eye as he twisted a foot on the cigarette. The gesture felt like the end of the conversation. I feared he might stop talking. He didn't. "The report claimed a mass grave was found by a couple of young lads a few years ago. Must be twenty years ago, now."

"Which young lads? Who?"

"My recollection is the boys were kicking football in the grounds of the Home when they came across a lump of concrete hidden in the grass. Curiosity got the better of them, as you'd expect from a couple of young fellas, and they lifted it." He took a deep breath. "They found a hole full of baby bones."

"Babies from the Home?"

"There's the debate. Babies from the Home, or a grave of young famine victims? No-one's sure."

"Fam–? Has it been investigated?"

"These things take time."

"Twenty years?"

"It's complicated."

"How complicated?"

Father Donal sighed. "There was concern at first. Local people visited, laid flowers, teddy bears, lullabies on cards. Anonymous tributes to anonymous children."

It sounded familiar. I quarried my memory. Mary's house. Were the bedroom-shrines entirely at Joe's insistence?

Father Donal Kealey stuffed his hands into pockets and stood still. "A local historian got interested and called for an analysis of the remains. It came to nothing. Newspapers and radio didn't pick up on it, and it blew over. Most didn't want to be talking about something like that ... A time best forgotten, maybe? It ended up declared a famine grave. There are thousands of them, all protected. An exhumation is a big step."

"So we've no way of confirming our daughter died? She may still be alive somewhere?"

"It's a possibility."

"Then we must look for her. We must seek her out. I'll look for her. Does Mary know all this?"

"I don't think so. *I* didn't tell her, anyhow."

"Why did you tell me?" I asked.

"I thought … I think you're the one to tell Mary. You both have a right to know. Father Brendan thinks you've a right to know. And he asks that you try to handle the Australian's situation sensitively."

"Jesus." I wanted a cigarette. I wanted a drink. "What about Sligo? Paul's birth certificate says 'Sligo'. Why?"

"For babies born in the Homes, the authorities weren't obliged to enter the name of the county of birth on the birth record. In fact, it safeguarded anonymity if they didn't. I've no idea why Paul's says 'Sligo'. False information can be more misleading than no information, it might have been Father Brendan protecting the girls. Or it might have been put there as a clue."

I rolled my back against the jagged wall of the barn and shook my head. The pain behind my eyes rocked from side to side. I gnawed at the remnants of a thumb nail.

"You've pledged to keep what I've told you quiet," Father Donal said. "Until Father Brendan passes. After that it's your choice, but until then…"

I wrung my hands together, pulling and crushing the fingers until they pained. "I don't know what to do with this."

"Talk to your family," Father Donal said. "Talk to Mary." He adjusted his hat. "That might be all you need to do with it. Ever. Or you can write a book."

I searched his face for a sign of humour. There was none. I thought of Mary. Of Joe and Mary. Of our daughter and Mary. I decided to look for our daughter.

Niamh and Paul had their backs to the window, leaning against the sink. Paul had an arm draped over the shoulders of his half-sister, her head curled into him.

I eased myself off the outbuilding, found my feet, and took two steadying breaths. I trudged through the blossom towards the house.

THE END.

Acknowledgements

I am grateful for information provided by the following: Adoption Rights Alliance, Mother and Baby Homes, The Guardian, The Mirror, The Independent, The Irish Examiner.

I owe a debt of gratitude to those who advised on content or took it upon themselves to read through and feedback on early drafts: Joan Carey, Paul McCormack, David Sykes, Jem Lough, Ellen Lessner, Eamonn O'Sullivan, Rebecca Reed, Lorraine Morrell, Don Bracken and Jim Adams R.I.P. Thank you all.

There is a group of writers in Banbury who also read through sections of the manuscript. Their criticisms and encouragements were invaluable.

The storyline is fictitious. So too are all the characters. Where I have used the names of real people from history the storyline has no connection with them in any way.

I am particularly grateful for reader reviews. Please post a review of *Sins of the Mothers* on the book's Amazon page.

Dennis Carey

About the Author

Dennis Carey was born in County Mayo, Ireland. His family moved to Coventry, England when he was very young.

He worked in education for 30 years, teaching for a short while in Secondary schools and more substantially in Further Education.

He lives with his wife in Northamptonshire, England.

Connect with Dennis Carey

Post a review on Amazon.
Twitter: http://twitter.com/dmpcarey
Email: sinsofthemothers@gmail.com
Like and comment on the *Sins of the Mothers* book page on Facebook
Connect on LinkedIn.

Also by Dennis Carey

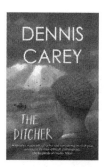

The Ditcher   Amazon Reviews:

***** A wonderfully written debut.
***** A really interesting book that I could not put down.
***** ...a totally absorbing and enjoyable read.
***** This is a terrific read.
***** I found the language authentic and the descriptions of the environment and the culture captivating.

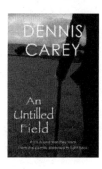

An Untilled Field   Amazon Reviews:

***** Compulsive Reading! The characters and storyline are compelling.
***** That was exactly how it was. Great read.
***** This is a wonderful book, could not put it down.
***** A must read! Within the first few chapters I was hooked. The character descriptions made them so real and I couldn't wait to find out if the boys were ok.
***** A fantastic read, I did not want to put the book down

Made in the USA
Columbia, SC
23 December 2017